Algoma Land

Algoma!

The new Ontario!! The new northwest!!! Happy homes and fertile farms!

Land for the landless! Homes for the homeless! - Algoma farmers testify

Algoma Land

Algoma!
*The new Ontario!! The new northwest!!! Happy homes and fertile farms! Land for
the landless! Homes for the homeless! - Algoma farmers testify*

ISBN/EAN: 9783337409142

Printed in Europe, USA, Canada, Australia, Japan

Cover: Foto ©Andreas Hilbeck / pixelio.de

More available books at **www.hansebooks.com**

ALGOMA

New Ontario. The New Northwest.

The Colonization and Immigration Movement in Algoma.

An Appeal to the Press.

DEAR SIR:

This great District of Algoma, (miscalled a *District*, in area and undeveloped resources a *Province*), although it contains millions of acres of the finest agricultural stock raising and fruit growing lands in the world, although there is room within its confines for the surplus population, not only of older Canada, and of the older of the United States, but of Europe, and although it is the nearest and most accessible field of Immigration and Colonization in the world to-day, lying as it does in the very centre of Canada, and being within twenty-four hours journey by rail or steamer from almost any part of older Ontario or Quebec, has never attracted any attention as a field of immigration or Colonization. Governments have given it the "go by."

Manitoba and the Northwest Territories have been largely and expensively "boomed" and advertised, but not a word has been said about this great count-

rich as it is, not only in agricultural stock raising, and fruit growing lands, but in minerals timber, and fisheries, and lying within twenty-four hours journey from Toronto or Montreal.

Not only have the Governments of Canada and of Manitoba spent immense sums in advertising the Canadian Northwest, but the C. P. R., and other corporations and Colonization Companies have for years been "booming" that part of the Dominion.

As Loyal Canadians we are glad to see our sister Provinces in the Canadian Northwest prosper and progress, but is it fair, has it been fair, to say all that has been said about their resources and inducements, and to say nothing about Algoma?

And above all and as loyal Canadians we deeply deplore the fact that thousands of well to do Canadians are and have been for years leaving the older Provinces of Canada and emigrating to the United States.

They are and have been for years passing over the various lines of railway by the carload, and by the lakes and rivers, by the ship load, going away from Canada to foreign states.

This is the "exodus" politicians tell us about. No matter what the political cause of it may be, (we leave that to the politicians on both sides of the House) this "exodus" does exist. Canadians go away thinking they will better their condition. As a fact in the majority of instances they do NOT better their condition, but greatly the reverse. And in connection with this "exodus" we ask the Governments at Ottawa and Toronto to call the attention of Canadians to the many and great inducements which this part of CANADA,—"The New Northwest," —this part of ONTARIO,—"The New Ontario"—offers to the intending colonist or settler; inducements and opportunities which lie so close at hand.

We are confident that if public attention were called to these facts the "exodus" would cease and not only that—a large immigration would commence to come into Algoma from Europe and older Canada, and better still, many Canadians sojourning in the United States would come back to Canada, to "New Ontario, the New Northwest," and so help to increase the wealth and prosperity of Canada.

Are we asking anything unreasonable? Should it not be the object of every loyal Canadian to foster a national sentiment, and try and keep "Canada for the Canadians"—and the Canadians in Canada.

As to European immigration:

There are thousands of tenant farmers in England, Ireland and Scotland, who toil on from year to year, and work hard, and never can get on, and then all their lives they remain LANDLESS. It is a fact that any English farmer can buy outright out—own absolutely—and stock—a good farm in Algoma of one hundred and sixty acres, with the same capital it would require simply to STOCK a farm in England of one hundred acres. After stocking his English farm he would not OWN it.

Would it not be well for the Governments of Canada and Ontario to make this known in Great Britain?

We have room within the confines of this great District for the landless folks, not only of older Canada, but of Europe. Would it not pay the Dominion and Ontario Governments to advertise this fact throughout the world? Is it not to the interest of both Governments to do so? Is not Algoma "The New Ontario" part of Ontario? Is not Algoma, "The New Northwest" part of Canada?

In addition to help us attract immigration from England, Ireland and Scotland, would it not be advisable for both Governments to help us publish literature and pamphlets about the agricultural, stock raising, and fruit growing resources of Algoma, in the German and Scandinavian languages, and help us circulate them in Germany, Norway, Sweden and Denmark? The Germans and Scandinavians make excellent, hard working settlers, and have largely aided in building up the American western and northwestern states.

Recognizing the fact that unless we made ourselves a big effort in the matter to help ourselves, we would never get "fair play" from the Governments, and recognizing the fact that being weighty, ponderous bodies, they move slowly, and that it takes a big effort generally to get them moving at all, a few energetic residents of the District met together last winter, and decided to take vigorous steps to bring Algoma prominently before the attention of the world as a desirable field of immigration. The gentlemen who thus took the matter in hand, were prominent men in the District, and all connected with the different Agricultural Societies and Farmers' Institutes in the District, and from their number an Executive Committee was chosen consisting of the following gentlemen; A. G. Duncan Esq., Late Crown Lands Agent for St. Josephs' Island, License Inspector for the District. D. Bole Esq., one of the License Commissioners for the District, and Fred Rogers Esq., B. C. L., a Director of the Eastern Algoma Electoral District Agricultural Society.

Since then everything possible has been done to help on the good cause. Large gatherings or mass meetings have been held all over the District, both on the North Shore and on the large and fertile islands of Manitoulin and St. Joseph. These meetings were largely "experience meetings;"—old settlers told of what they had successfully accomplished in the District, and compared it with other localities in Canada, Europe or the United States, where they had formerly lived. Valuable facts, figures and statistics were thus gathered for publication. One good effect of these meetings has been that great interest in the cause of immigration and colonization has been aroused all over the District.

To prove this we may call attention to the fact that the grand juries at the recent Assizes and General Sessions held throughout the District, have in their several Presentments referred to the movement and heartily endorsed it, and recited the injustice done to the District by the neglect of the Governments in the premises, and strongly urged upon the Governments of the Dominion and the Province at once to adopt a vigorous immigration policy with respect to "Algoma, the New Ontario; the New Northwest." Certified copies of these Presentments as well as of the strong resolutions passed at the different mass meetings, have been forwarded to the Governments at Ottawa and Toronto, as well as long petitions, (setting forth all the facts in connection with the whole matter) from and signed by all the Public and Representative bodies in the District, the different municipal corporations, Agricultural Societies, Boards of trade, Farmers Institutes, etc.

If petitioning by public and representative bodies is of any use Algoma should get "fair play" in immigration and colonization matters at once. But as we say Governments are slow to move, and there are no politics involved. The petition from the public bodies to the Ontario Government amongst other matters sets forth as follows:

"WHEREAS the District of Algoma contains millions of acres of valuable agricultural and stock raising lands,

AND whereas, owing to the District being situated along the great water highway of commerce, farmers and settlers in Algoma can never be at the mercy of railways or of "combines" as in other portions of the country, and in this respect alone Algoma offers particular inducements for settlement, as, in addition to being on the route of several lines of steamers and sailing vessels (the tonnage of which is yearly increasing) the District is traversed by two main lines operated by the Canadian Pacific Railway Company (the main line proper, and the "Sault Short Line" from Minneapolis to Boston), and several other railways are chartered both by the Dominion and Ontario Governments to run through the District,

AND whereas there is and always will be, owing to the large public works in the District, and to the lumbering and mining operations, a good and very remunerative market right at the farmer's own door so to speak, a "home market" for all the farmer or stock raiser can grow or raise,

AND whereas the Fairs held annually not only by the Eastern Algoma Electoral District Agricultural Society at Sault Ste. Marie, but also by the different township agricultural societies throughout the District prove conclusively that Algoma possesses the greatest possible agricultural and stock raising resources,

AND whereas all settlers who have come to Algoma and ..... their farms and worked industriously have done exceedingly well, althou.. unlike other countries, no farmers or stock raisers have ever come to this l.. t with any means or capital at all, or with any practical knowledge of agricult.. or stock raising as a science or profession.

AND whereas Algoma offers the greatest possible induce..... tenant farmers and others from older lands who have a little means or cap.. h..wever comparatively small, and a practical knowledge of farming.

AND whereas any settler in Algoma can testify to the followi.. t.. 1) The abundance of good water all through the District—creeks, sprin... .. s, etc, (2) The absence of drought or of summer frosts; the absenc.. .. .. ards in winter, and hurricanes in summer or grasshoppers, which are such gr..t .. wbacks in Dakota, the Western and Northwestern States. (3) The fertility of the soil and the rapid growth in summer. (4) The abundance of good wood and timber of various kinds all over the District. (5) The fact that directly the sn w goes off in the spring, the grass is green, and that sheep and cattle can pastur outside in the woods and commons, etc, till very late in the fall, or early in th winter; that the grass and herbage does not wither or get brown and parched through the summer as in other countries, and that cattle and sheep do extreme ly well, and will thrive running wild anywhere on the wild grass and herbag which grows so luxuriantly through the District everywhere; that, in addition to the large profit which can be made here in the pursuit of general agricultu re, this country offers the greatest inducements for cattle and sheep rais.. ..t.. on the high lands and the rocky bluffs and ridges which, here and ther.. are ..und in the District, sheep can be successfully pastured all spring, summer nd fall without any cost; that the rocky ridges and bluffs, which occu here an l there, are covered with grass and herbage very suitable and nourishing for sh ep, and that white clover is indigenous to the soil and grows everywhere. An l t there are thousands of acres of magnificent lands along the different rivers suitable for ranching or pasturing cattle. (6) That wheat (spring and fall) d..es ex ..dingly well here, and yields large crops; that oats, barley, peas and other crops also do extremely well and yield largely. (7) That the hay crop is enormous, and that we know of no country where larger and better crops of hay can be grown. (8) That roots of all kinds—potatoes, turnips, mangolds, etc.—do exceedingly well, better than we have seen anywhere else. (9) That garden.. g pays here; that everything which can be, or usually is, grown in a garden can be su cessfully grown here, and with a large profit. (10) That fruits of differen.. k.. ds can be grown here in abundance; that the strawberry, raspberry, huckleberry, cr..nb rry, etc., grows here, wild, in abundance; that currants of the different k.. d.. well here, also plums, cherries, apples and crab-apples, and that a f.. mer stock raiser coming to Algoma with a little means and a practical knowledg.. .. f..rm ng would be better off in Algoma in TWO years than he would be in D.. .. .. the North-west or the South or West of the United States in TEN yea.. .. f..rther, by coming here he would escape a great many hardships and priv.. .. he would find here roads, schools, churches, stores, etc., and would not have to undergo a great many of the privations which the pioneer in other countries had to endure,

AND whereas the District of Algoma contains an area greater than most of the Provinces of Canada or the States of the Union,

AND whereas the District of Algoma is in the centre of Canada; and is the nearest and most accessible field of immigration and colonization in the world to-day, and is easily and cheaply reached,

AND whereas it all belongs to the Province of Ontario, "The Banner Province of the Dominion."

AND whereas it is to the interest of the Province of Ontario that this great District, which is part and parcel of Ontario, should be settled,

AND whereas there are in the District of Algoma, and belonging to the Ontario Government, a great many townships of free grant and 20c. an acre land open for settlement, and a great many other townships not yet open for settlement, all containing as fine agricultural and stock raising land as the sun shines on anywhere,

AND whereas the country lying between the Pancake River in the township of Ryan on the west, and the Mississauga River in the township of Thompson on the east, is a stretch of agricultural country some 160 miles in length and is a succession of valleys watered by the Pancake, Batchewana, Goulais, several branches of the Root, Garden, Echo, Stobie, Bar, Thessalon, Mississauga and other rivers, and affords a stretch of magnificent agricultural and stock raising lands capable, within itself, of containing the farming population of a province, and even east of the Mississauga on the Spanish river, and on the fertile islands of St. Joseph, Cockburn and Manitoulin, and in the Rainy River District, and the township of Oliver and other portions of Thunder Bay district, there are thousands of acres of magnificent farming and stock raising lands.

AND whereas it is to the interest of the Province of Ontario to adopt a vigorous immigration policy, and settle this "New Ontario," this "New Northwest."

AND whereas the Provincial Government of the Province of Manitoba, although young province and a poor province compared with the Province of Ontario, has been and is spending thousands and thousands of dollars yearly on immigration matters,

AND whereas the Government of the Province of Ontario has not spent one cent in helping to settle this great District of Algoma, which is part and parcel of Ontario, and has done nothing to make known to the world its many and great agricultural and stock raising resources,

AND whereas if Algoma had had fair play in this direction, if she had had one tenth part of the chance other countries, not nearly so deserving it, have had; if she had had any chance at all, she would be, to-day, not thinly and sparsely settled, but thickly settled, rich and prosperous.

AND whereas, within the last few years, millions of emigrants and settlers have come to this continent from Great Britain, Germany and the Scandinavian Countries, and have built up the Western States and Territories, and the Western Provinces and Territories,

AND whereas these settlers and emigrants are still coming by thousands yearly to this continent,

AND whereas there is in this great District of Algoma room for the surplus population of Europe,

AND whereas thousands of the young men of Ontario, the flower of the country, besides thousands of older men have within the last few years been induced to leave the Province of Ontario and settle in the Western States and Territories, and Manitoba, and the Northwest Territories of Canada,

AND whereas they are still leaving this province every year to the great hurt and detriment of this Province of Ontario; this Province of Ontario is in this way getting depopulated of its best and strongest element of strength, the young and middle aged farmers,

AND whereas there are thousands of the young men of Ontario, farmer's sons who have become unsettled through reading, and hearing so much about the Western States and Manitoba, and the Northwest Territories,

AND whereas the District of Algoma contains a vast area of the finest agricultural and stock raising lands in the world lying right side by side with a vast area of rich mineral lands,

AND whereas this great District "New Ontario, the New Northwest" is part and parcel of Ontario, the "Banner Province" of the Dominion,

AND whereas these young men and middle aged men from older Ontario by coming and settling in Algoma will not be leaving the Province or breaking up their old homes, as they will be within a days journey by rail or steamer from their old homes,

AND whereas by coming and settling in Algoma they will become a large source of strength and wealth to the Province of Ontario and largely increase its prosperity instead of leaving the Province and building up a foreign or an alien State, or adding to the wealth of another Canadian Province; as the Algoma Advocate recently remarks:—"Manitoba is attracting settlers in large numbers from Ontario. They are evidently appreciated, for the Winnipeg Tribune remarks:—'After all it is the trained farmers from Ontario that Manitoba wants, and we are getting a good slice of them this season. One good Ontario farmer located in Manitoba is worth a dozen English emigrants who know nothing about conditions here, and who, after failing to make a living, generally leave the country with a curse. A hardy Ontario farmer who is able to battle with the difficulties encountered in pioneer farming, is just the kind of settler Manitoba needs.' Why is it that people will go thousands of miles from their old homes and associations to settle, when they can secure good homes for themselves and families at their own doors (in Algoma) is puzzling; Ontario's loss is Manitoba's gain."

"AND whereas all that needs to be done to lead to this District being thickly and quickly settled is to advertise throughout the world its many, and great agricultural, and stock raising advantages, inducements and resources."

The one to the Dominion Government among other matters emphasizes the fact that there are in the District of Algoma belonging to the Dominion Government a great many townships both on the Main Land and the Great Manitoulin and Cochburn Islands, Surrendered Indian Lands, (Dominion Crown Lands) all containing as fine agricultural stock raising and fruit growing lands as the sun shines on anywhere.

The Executive Committee have also encouraged the settlers throughout the District to start and write letters to the different newspapers and journals published in the different localities in Europe, Canada or the United States, from wherever they came to Algoma—letters stating their personal experience and success in Algoma. The result of all this agitation has been that a feeling of great interest in the matter [is being awakened all over Ontario, Quebec and the Maritime Provinces. Among a good many editorials which have recently appeared in prominent newspapers published outside the District, the following shows what the Toronto daily papers think about the movement.

CHEAP FARMS IN ONTARIO.

TORONTO DAILY NEWS.

"Those who are casting about for a new place of abode should not lose sight of the great territory included in the electoral district of Eastern Algoma.

Enormous advantages are offered in this new territory. The Climate is unsurpassed; the country is well watered; there is abundance of timber; the soil is peculiarly well adapted for the production of roots and hay; fruits of the hardier varieties yield abundantly; and there is, owing to the large lumbering and mining industries carried on, always an unlimited demand for labor and a home market at high prices for everything a farmer can produce. Owing to the abundance of water and the adaptability of the soil for roots, coarse grain and grass, the district is particularly well suited for stock raising and dairying, and already this industry has reached considerable proportions. The means of communication with the outside world are good, the Sault branch of the Canadian Pacific running right through the territory, and several steamers touching at the various ports. Land is cheap, good farms being obtainable at prices ranging from $300 to $1,500. Although, as stated, the schools are necessarily somewhat backward and roads not of the best, still both are far ahead of those provided for the early settlers in the older parts of Ontario. Few of the residents are more than three miles from a school, and it is a comparatively common thing to drive a buckboard over sixty miles of the country roads in a day.

Altogether, those young farmers who are turning their eyes to Manitoba might do well to look first, at a district that can be reached in twenty-four hours from Toronto. And it is a question, too, if even some of those who are rushing away from the cities in search of a boom in Buffalo or Chicago, could not better provide for their families by securing a farm in Algoma than they can by plunging into the big centers of the United States."

WHY GO TO THE FAR WEST.

TORONTO DAILY MAIL.

"When so many farmers are leaving Ontario to go westward it is worthy of note that this Province has a few acres still unsettled. So far the district of Algoma has not attracted immigration to a large extent, but in the opinion of those who live there it can offer good inducements to agriculturists. At a recent public meeting in Gore Bay the advantages of the locality for settlers were unanimously affirmed by resolution.

The district was declared to have an immense area of fine agricultural and stock raising lands, besides vast mineral and timber resources, easily reached and convenient to good markets. The Dominion and Provincial Governments were urged to assist the special efforts of the residents in securing settlers. The prayer should fall on willing ears. Those who do not know that distant fields always look the greenest will not be deterred from going to the far west, but there are others who prefer not to go far from their old home, and to such Algoma may offer tempting inducements.

Every day or two similar editorials are appearing in the different leading newspapers in the older parts of Ontario.

The Executive Committee are also preparing and collecting exhibits of grain grown in the District showing the stalk and also exhibits of the woods and timber grown in the District for exhibition in Great Britain and at the World's Fair in Chicago.

The Committee are also offering prizes to be competed for at the next Annual Fall Show of the Eastern Algoma Electoral District Agricultural Society which will be held at Sault Ste. Marie on the 4th, 5th, and 6th days of October next for the three best essays written by the farmer's wives and daughters of Algoma descriptive of "Farm Life in 'Algoma, The New Ontario, The New Northwest.'" "Algoma as a suitable field for Immigration and Colonization, and the home of the intending settler—its advantages and inducements."

During the last few months the Executive Committee have been busy collecting fact and figures from farmers, stock raisers, dairymen and millers all over the North Shore, and the large and fertile Islands of St. Josephs Cockburn and Manitoulin and the information and statistics they have gathered is something immense and go to prove conclusively that Algoma offers greater inducements and opportunities to the intending settler or colonist than any other field of immigration in the world can possibly offer.

What the people of the District ask the Dominion and Ontario Governments to do is to grant our Executive Committee at once sufficient money to enable them to print and circulate throughout Canada and Great Britain pamphlets containing the information and statistics they have gathered as the result of their labors and to furnish them; also sufficient funds to publish and circulate French, German and Scandinavian editions of the same pamphlets.

Circulars asking for information and statistics have been sent to every settler and other person likely to be able to give reliable information, and a good many settlers all over the District have been interviewed personally. The letters and statements thus obtained are all in the settler's own language and their very wording and language prove the sincerity and truth of the writers one would almost think. The collecting of all these statistics, letters statements and information of one kind and another, and the holding of public meetings all over the District and the large amount of other work done by the members of the Committee in connection with the Immigration and Colonization movement have of course cost a large amount of valuable time and money.

Among other printed matter circulated through the District a document entitled "Algoma Farmers Testify" has been filled up signed and returned to the Executive Committee by hundreds of settlers.

It reads "we have much pleasure in stating that we sincerely believe Algoma to-day offers the best and greatest inducements possible to farmers and colonists seeking to make a comfortable home for themselves. We confidently believe that any man willing to work and having a practical knowledge of farming or stock raising can do well here, and get on even if he has no money or very little, there being abundance of work in the winter months in the lumber camps, mines, etc., and especially do we believe that the fertile District of Algoma offers the greatest possible inducements to a farmer or a stock raiser having a little means or small capital however comparatively small, and a practical knowledge of farming. There is, and we believe always will be a good home market here for every thing a farmer or stock raiser can grow or raise. We believe the market prices here are and always will be higher than any where else. We all of us can testify to the following facts :

Then follows (1) to (10) as printed above, (ante pages 5 and 6,) and then it proceeds: We have much pleasure in stating that we will be willing to answer any enquiries which may be made of us us to the great agricultural and stock raising resources of Algoma.

NAME.	P. O. ADDRESS & TOWNSHIP (ALGOMA.)	HOW LONG IN ALGOMA.	WHERE ENGAG- ED IN FARMING BEFORE.	REMARKS.
				State anything you think may be of interest and not contained in above. We wish you to state under this head anything which may give information to the intending colonist or immigrant.

The information gathered from "Algoma Farmers Testify" alone is very interesting and conclusive. The people who have signed it hail from all parts of the world. Under the head of "Remarks," there are scores of people who write in this strain in their own handwriting:

"Land fertile. Yields wheat, peas and oats. Roots of all kinds do well. Have made more money here in half the time than I ever made in the county of York, and the climate healthier."

"Land fertile. Grows good grain of all kinds, grows good roots also. The very best fruits such as cherries, plums, currants and apples. Cattle and sheep do extra well here. Have a large number of bees which do well also. I have handled bees for forty years and never seen them do as well." This man also hails from York county.

"I like the District better than I ever liked Norfolk. Have done well here. Made more property in one year than I ever made in my life. Want more settlers."

"I am getting along well for a man of small means. I don't know where I could go to get along better if I was going to farm."

"Like the country well. Which is the best I know for stock raising as well as grain of all kinds. Came from Township Vespera.

"A miller says: "Have been running a grist mill for a number of years and find the farmers doing well in this part, and also find quality of grain grown first-class."

A man from **Pickering, Ontario,** says: "Can grow good crops of grain and roots or garden stuff. Have made a good living from the first."

"I like the Island well for its good climate, and its great grain growing facilites. '

Another says: "I like the Island well. Can do better here than I ever did before I came. I came from Simcoe county.

"No place a good man can do better in that I know of. Came from Artemesia."

"I am satisfied with this place for farming and stock raising. I grow as good fall wheat and crops of all kinds as in the county of York which supposed to be the finest farming county in the Province of Ontario

"Come from the county of Wellington. That country is noted for stock raising and farming in general and I think this is equal to that county.

"I find this District second to none in the world for mixed farming."

"Came from county of Bruce, Township of Ammabel. I now live in Rose Township, Algoma. Rose Township is excellent for both cattle and sheep raising, any amount of wild pasture. I think sheep raising would be very profitable in Rose Township. Sheep and cattle can run wild through the woods and wild commons and beaver meadows. There are any number of little springs, and creeks (containing speckled trout) all over Rose Township, Algoma. I have two orchards planted, both doing well, big healthy trees. Apples are going to be a great success. I believe in a few years Algoma will be a good apple country, if the farmers will start and plant out orchard."

"My expenses left me in debt when I came here with my wife and five children. Now I am well off. Thank God for it. N. B.: I have a horse and buggy free for my own use. Came from Warwichshire, England. Address, Tenby Bay, St. Joseph's Island."

"Come from Hastings, Ontario. I am well satisfied with this place for farming and stock raising. Came here with hardly any money at all, and would not take less than $1,000 for stock and property.

"Came from Wellington county. Well pleased with St. Joseph's Island and doing well."

Another man writes that he came from the state of Michigan, and adds: "After having travelled over all the Western States in search of a home, I came here with small means. I am now doing well with a good stock of cattle, sheep and horses of my own and thank God all paid for. I prefer this place to any other."

Another man who came from Ontario county, says: "Peas 52, Oats 40, Wheat 30, Buckwheat 25 bushels per acre, this grown on my place.

"I am doing well and am contented. Came from Ottawa.

"Came from Cartwright. "60 bushels of Oats, 20 Wheat, 50 Peas to the acre. I grow good apples and other fruit. Am doing well.

"The above statements are not over drawn (referring to (1) to (10.)

"The above statements are not near as strong as I would have put them (referring to 1 to 10.)

"I have been in a great many parts of the country, but I have not seen any place yet to beat Algoma. We have no failure of crops, and a healthy climate. Came from Middlesex.

"Climate particularly adapted for stock."

"Well adapted for stock."

"Have raised the best wheat here I ever did.

(Two men make the above assertion, and sign opposite it, one from county Elgin, and the other from county Waterloo.)

"Four men now living on St. Joseph's Island and originally coming from Middlesex, Wellington, Oxford and Fontenac, respectively put a bracket opposite the following: "This is a fine farming country and is a sportsman's paradise, abounding with all kinds of game and fish."

"A miller says: "I feel satisfied that Algoma is fully equal to Eastern Ontario for mixed farming. All kinds of grain do well here. Grass can not be beaten, we can raise better grass fed beef in Algoma than can be produced in any part of Ontario (or Canada.) As for grain I never milled better wheat than I have done in Algoma. I made quite a number of tests from farmers grists during the winter, and seldom found a test go below sixty pounds per bushel, and some as high as sixty-five pounds per bushel. For the vicinity of Port Lock, on the North Shore between Bruce Mines and Sault Ste. Marie, spring wheat averages from twenty to twenty-five bushels per acre, fall or winter wheat twenty-five to thirty bushels per acre. Pease are easily grown, and are a sure crop. They average about forty bushel per acre. Oats are generally a good crop. All kinds of root crops grow well here. I have known potatoes to yield fifty bushels from one bushel planted. I feel so well satisfied with Algoma and with the prospects for the future, that I have no desire to return to Eastern Ontario.

A St. Joseph's Island man, says: "I came here thirteen years ago without any money or hardly any, and did not know anything about the bush. Now I have fifty acres of cleared land, and a good stock of cattle and a team of horses."

Another man from the same Island says: "I have worked around mines and on railroads and had good pay, but could not save any money until I came to St. Joseph's Island. When I came I had one cow, and about $50 in cash. Now I am worth $2,000 and I am only here 14 years."

"Others say: "Been over the most of Canada and the States and St. Joseph's Island is the best place I have seen for a man with small means. Never saw a place where crops grew better."

"I came here four years ago. Had $700. Now I am worth $2,000. My P. O. is Carterton."

"I came here thirteen years ago. I did not have $5. Now I have three hundred acres of good land, one horse, one yoke of oxen and a good stock of sheep, cattle and pigs. I think St. Joseph's Island is the place to settle in.

"I came here ten years ago. I only had $1 when I landed at the dock. Now have two hundred acres of land, and am doing well. Algoma is the place for a poor man, or a man with some capital.

"I got a free grant lot 13 years ago and then had only 1 horse, 1 cow and no money. Now I have 3 horses, 5 cows and a good stock of young cattle, 6 sheep, 3 pigs, 30 hens, a mowing machine, wagon, harrow, plow, good house, a bank barn 36x60, thirty acres cleared and don't owe any man a dollar."

"I came to St. Joseph 6 years ago was $300. in debt when I came here. By this spring I have cleared myself of debt, and have in addition got stock and cattle around me of my own, and good land of my own; am doing well, satisfied and contented."

"I used to farm in Co. Elgin, Ontario. Elgin is considered one of the best fall wheat counties of Canada. I have on St. Joseph Island better fall wheat than I ever saw or grew in Elgin Co., or that I ever saw anywhere. If anyone thinks good fall wheat cannot be grown in Algoma he is mistaken."

A dairyman says in an interesting letter too long to publish here in full. "I live in township Tarentorus, 3 miles from the town of Sault Ste. Marie. Have been 12 years in Algoma, and can speak from experience as to its climate. I came from Norfolk, England. There is lots of money in stock raising in Algoma; from early summer till late in the fall cattle can run wild and do well. Can run wild anywhere and cost nothing for their keep. Hay is a good crop; I often have from 2 tons to 2½ tons to the acre. Turnips grow good, carrots also; in fact the roots can't be beat. I never saw better samples of roots anywhere than I see every fall at the District Fall show at Sault Ste. Marie. Fruit does well in Algoma; strawberries and all small fruits do extremely well. Wild strawberries and raspberries are abundant. Any of the townships around Sault Ste. Marie would make a good home for the intending settler, if he will work hard and attend to his business; to succeed a man must work anywhere and the more a man knows practically about farming and dairying the better he can do, the more money he can make. A man coming here without any money if he works hard and has a knowledge of the business, can perhaps get on better in Algoma than in other countries where there is no work or employment in the winter months as there is in Algoma in the woods and mines and on public works; but the kind of farmers to come here and the men who would make themselves independently well off in a very short time, are tenant farmers and others with a little means or capital and a good practical knowledge of farming or stock raising; men who understand it as a business and who have a little money to buy good stock and implements and get well started. The farmers now in Algoma came without money. I came here 12 years ago without any money at all I don't think I had $12 when I landed at the Sault Ste. Marie dock. There was no railway here then. If the farmers who are going to Dakota and the Northwest with $1000 and upwards, would come here they would do better and be better off I believe in 2 years in Algoma, than they would be in Dakota or the Northwest in 10 years, and they would escape many hardships My post office address is Sault Ste Marie; will be glad to answer any inquiries which may be made of me personally or by mail.

And so on; scores of them but too long to publish here. Among others a very interesting one from a gentleman, Reeve of his township, who was engaged in sheep raising in Roxborough, Scotland, and Australia, and who compared Algoma favorably with both countries. "I understand sheep raising have followed it all my life. Since I have been in Burpee township I have never known a case of "foot rot" in Algoma nor "liver worms." I don't know of any sheep disease or cattle disease in Algoma. I never knew cattle or sheep to die in Algoma except from accident. Without doubt I believe this is the healthiest place for stock of all kinds and sheep. In fact speaking generally I think Algoma the healthiest climate in the world; the winters I consider very healthy both for man and stock and sheep. The air is exhilarating and dry in winter. In summer it is never very hot, the nights are always cool, and very heavy dews as a general thing. One cause why the climate is moist In summer is the presence of so much fresh water in and all around Algoma. The big lakes—really inland seas—and so many inland rivers, lakes and streams. There is abundance of good water for man and beast. The moist temperature keeps the grass and herbage green and luxurant all summer."

This gentleman enlarges at length on the fact of the clover being indigenous to the soil and the great advantage it is to sheep raising.

He says further: "Industrious men have always succeeded here even if they had no capital, and I can tell you dozens of them in Algoma. As to fruit, I have a good orchard of apples (some are seedlings grafted by me and some are from nurseries) plums and cherries; they are all thrifty trees. My trees have been bearing for some years."

There is a very interesting letter from a lady farmer in Tarbutt town-

ship. She came from Worcestershire, England. The letter shows the money there is to be made in Algoma out of the dairy business alone. We wish we could publish the letter in full. Among other things she says:—
"I lived in Worcestershire, England; it was a good grazing country. I don't think the seasons here in Algoma are any shorter than they are in the Midland counties of England. We commenced to stable our cattle in Tarbutt township in Algoma about Christmas, last year about the 1st. of January, and we let them out again about the 15th of April.

The kind of farmers who should come here in my opinion and who would do well here are the working tenant farmers of England. Farmers who have capital in England to work a 100 acre farm, could buy and stock in this country a good 'farm of 160 acres. That is I mean, the capital which would be needed to work a farm in England of 100 acres would buy outright and well stock a farm of 160 acres in Algoma, either on the main land, or the Islands; and furthermore, there is already a valuable crop already planted by nature; I mean the valuable timber of different kinds, hardwood and soft wood, pulp (paper fiber wood.) This is one of the advantages of farming in a timbered country. I would not want to live in a prairie country. In a prairie country you have no timber; you have to buy any you need. Here when one goes on a farm you find valuable timber of all kinds. There are a good many other reasons why a timbered country should be preferred to a prairie country. The timber is a great protection against the wind also; we have no blizzards in winter or hurricanes in summer, and we have excellent and sweet spring water for man or beast. I like the climate both in summer and winter and would not want to live anywhere else.

A tenant farmer in England can never get ahead and he can't keep out of debt. * * * * If anyone doubts what I say let them write me to McLennan post office, or come to my farm in Tarbutt. My nearest steamship port is Port Finlay about 2 miles from my farm; nearest railway station is Tarbut Crossing on the Sault branch of the C. P. R., about 4 miles from my farm. I will be glad to give or write any information I can to intending settlers either from England or Canada."

There are dozens of similar letters from people all over the north shore and the islands. Among others some very interesting ones from the Goulais Bay, Prince, Pennefather and Korah settlements northwest of Sault Ste.

Marie, and from the Thessalon district east of the Sault. Lots of the letters deal with the fruit question and clearly prove that if the farmers will start and plant orchards of the hardy kind of trees, in a few years Algoma will be exporting apples. To any one interested in fruit growing we will be happy to send copies or exracts from the letters.

And then the claims of Algoma as a summer resort, and as a place of healthful residence, at all times of the year should not be forgotten. Especially during the heated term. There are several lines of steamers running through the "inside" channel. If you want to see the District take one of the "local" steamers from Collingwood, Wiarton. or Owen Sound, not the "through" steamers. These "local steamers" stop at ALL the ports in the District. Get off at any of these ports and stay there a few days or weeks, walk or drive back in the country and see for yourself what it is like. Bring your wife and children along. Bring your friends along. Rich milk and delicious cream are plentiful, and fresh eggs, and butter. Bring your fishing rod along, and your trolling hooks. There are lots of good hotels and private houses where you can stop if you don't want to camp out. You will find it preferable to going to some over crowded summer resort. Kagawong, Gore Bay, Thessalon (thence back to the lakes at Day Mills, a chain of beautiful inland lakes, Big Basswood, Little Basswood, Mud and Clear Lakes, affording splendid fishing, bathing and boating, and on to the Iron Bridge on the Mississauga River where the Govt. Road crosses this noble river by a magnificent iron structure.) Marksville, (Hilton Dock,) Richard's Landing, Sailor's Encampment, Sault Ste. Marie, Goulias River and lots of other places on the North Shore, and the Islands are well worth visiting and at any one of them probably you could find pleasant quarters for a few weeks' or months' stay and there are splendid farm lands round each of them. In fact you can find pleasant stopping places along the route of any of the "local" steamship lines running from Wiarton, Owen. Sound or Collingwood, or if your objective point is Sault Ste. Marie simply you can take the Beatty "through" line from Sarnia, Southampton, Kincardine or Goderich or the C. P. R. "through" steamers direct from Owen Sound to Sault Ste. Marie. In winter you can take "the Sault Branch" of the C. P. R. (really part of a main line between Boston and St. Paul and Duluth) or in summer you can return that way if in a hurry. Or in summer you can come, say by the inside channel (Local Route) and return by the outside channel. It is a wonder that so few Canadians visit the cool and refreshing regions of the St. Mary's River and the North Channel during " the heated term." We need not here say anything about the valuable fisheries of the District or about the great undeveloped mineral wealth of all kinds except to say that it is not generally known that Algoma is the only country in the world where large tracts of exceedingly rich minerals are found lying side by side with tracts of the richest agricultural stock raising and fruit growing lands. That here the PRODUCER and the CONSUMER can live side by side as it were.

Nor need we say any thing about the magnificent tracts of valuable merchantable maple and birch in the district or of the pulp (paper fibre) wood industry which is assuming such large proportions yearly in the district. Suffice it to say that in all lines of trade commerce and manufacture there is lots of room in Algoma, and there is no country in the world to-day that offers greater or safer inducements for the investment of capital in all lines of trade, industry or commerce, than does " Algoma, the New Ontario, the New Northwest."

During the last few days the members of the Executive Committee have received requests from newspaper men in different towns and cities in lower Ontario and Quebec to furnish them with information and data regarding the new Colonization and Immigration movement in Algoma, and we have thought it best to issue this circular and send it to every newspaper and journal in Ontario and to several of the leading newspapers in Quebec, the Maritime Provinces and Great Britain and Ireland.

We do this for your general information, and in conclusion ask you the members of the great Fourth Estate, knowing the great influence the press has and its mighty power for good in the world, and feeling that the cause we are championing is a good one and worthy of all assistance.

1. To publish gratuitously in the next edition of your valuable journal this circular in full; and if you have not space to publish it in full in one issue to publish part in one issue and part in another.

2. If your paper is a weekly as well as a daily newspaper we ask you to publish it in both the weekly and daily editions.

3. To use the influence of your valuable paper in endeavoring to get

the Dominion and Ontario Governments—each of them— to make immediate
liberal grants to our Executive Committee to enable us to pay for the printing
and circulation throughtout Canada, the United States and Europe, of
pamphlets descriptive of the agricultural, stock raising and fruit growing
resources of "Algoma, the New Ontario, the New Northwest," and to enable
us also to issue and circulate French, German and Scandinavin editions of
the same, and to induce both the Governments at once to adopt a vigorous
immigration policy with respect to this great District of Algoma.

4. To write and publish in your valuable paper from time to time,
editorials and editorial comments relating to the immigration movement in
Algoma, and the inducements and opportunities offered by this great District
as a desirable field of immigration and the home of the intending settler and
colonist.

5. To come up and see this great country for yourself at once, or send a
representative to see it and make a report or write a series of articles for
your paper. It would be a pleasant trip for you or your special reporter or
correspondent to make Come at any time of the year; in winter by rail
of course. If you come now fetch fishing tackle along with you. If you
have a "Kodak" handy fetch it along too. The scenery both on the north
shore and the islands is grand and picturesque, and has never been photo.
graphed—virgin soil for the camera. Never forget that a casket which has
a rough exterior may yet contain jewels of inestimable value. And in your
travels remember that while Algoma has a rough and rock-bound and
uninviting coast,—the exterior of the casket— yet if one travels a mile or
two back from the coast at any of the ports we have mentioned, or from
any of the railway stations on the Sault branch, between say the Mississauga
river and the Batchewana river and also on the Spanish river, he will find
tracts of arable agricultural and fruit growing lands and stock raising lands
as fine as the sun shines on anywhere. The deceptive and uninviting
appearance of the country from the deck of a steamer or a car window,
has aided largely in the non-settlement of this country—if we may use the
expression.

It is never safe in this world to judge entirely from appearances. We
think you can now find friends at almost any town, village or settlement in
the Electoral District who will tell you where and to whom to go for informa-

tion as to the agricultural, stock raising or fruit growing resources of the vicinity. At all our mass meetings held all over the country we have urged the people to be hospitable to "strangers" who may come "to view the land," and have reminded them that if the "strangers" happen to be newspaper men, they may be "entertaining angels unawares." If any of you drop us a line, we will send you letters of introduction to leading and influential residents in different parts of the District, many of whom have volunteered at our meetings to drive people around their neighborhoods and show them the country. We have had procured and printed for the advantage of newspaper men a circular letter of introduction addressed to leading people, merchants, officials and others residing at different places in the District, and if you are travelling in Algoma it may be of some service to you to have one of these circular letters of introduction with you. It may perhaps ensure you better accommodation, better information, better fishing, bathing and boating, and a better "time" generally. We will be glad to send you one if you drop us a card and we will not consider it any trouble.

6. Encourage Canadians to spend their summer vacations, in fact all their vacations at any time of the year, in Canada, and not go away to foreign countries and over heated and so called summer resorts, but to try Algoma either the north shore or the islands, a country within 24 hours ride of Montreal or Toronto, befor "going further and faring worse."

7. Do all you can to prevent a further "exodus" to the United States. Encourage Canadians in your vicinity who are seeking a new home for themselves or their sons to try "Algoma, the New Ontario, the New Northwest," before going to a foreign country where they will in all probability not only have to undergo privations and hardships, but in which they will not do as well in 10 years as they could in Algoma in 2 years, (as proof of this read our "Algoma Farmers Testify" and also what the signers of that document say under the head of "Remarks"). Try and keep Canada for the Canadians, and the Canadians in Canada. Why should Canadians try and build up Minnesota, North and South Dakota, Montana, Washington, Kansas, and other Western, Northwestern and Southwestern States?

8. Publish from time to time as they may be sent you any letters or

statements about this country written by the settlers in Algoma. We are encouraging them to write to the Canadian and British Press.

Apologizing for the length of this circular, and pleading the cause of duty as the only excuse for our otherwise unwarranted invasion of your "editorial sanctum." I am, Yours Faithfully,

FRED ROGERS, Secretary Executive Committee.

Sault Ste. Marie, Ontario.

APPENDIX.

ALGOMA FARMERS TESTIFY.

The following are the names and post office addresses of a few of the actual settlers in Algoma who have signed the document now in our possession and open to public inspection, "Algoma Farmers Testify." We have not space to publish all the names. There are scores of them all over the North Shore and the Islands. We have not space to publish their interesting "Remarks." They all ask people to correspond with them about Algoma. Don't be afraid to write any of them.

Thomas Bowser, (Reeve Municipality) Kagawong Postoffice, Billings township, 14 years in Algoma. Came from county of York, Ont.

Robert Bivett do 17, county York, Ont.

Donald McKenzie, do 14, did not farm before coming to Algoma.

George Waterhouse, do 14, did not farm before coming to Algoma.

Thomas F. Richards, 22, county Bruce, Ont.

Henry F. Ganan, do 22, Norfolk.

W. J. Holliday, (Agent for the estate of W. and R. Henry) 171 St. Clarence Ave,, Toronto, Ont.: "I have spent considerable time on the Island and have seen considerable of the same, and I find the farmers progressing. Consider it a good place for stock or mixed farming."

Donald Fraser, Billings township, Kagawong Postoffice, 13 years.

David Munro, do 12, county Simcoe.

T. J. Thompson, do 14, county Simcoe.

J. A. Wilson do 18, did not farm before coming here.

Benjamin Palmer, Campbell township, Providence Bay Postoffice, 8 years, Pickering, Ont.

J. C. Moore, Green Bay Postoffice, 8 years.

J. Newburn, Kagawong, 13.

Wm. Snow, do 30 years before coming here.

William Bailie, Kagawong, 16 years, Simcoe county.

James McGawley, (Mun. Councillor) 15, Artemesia.

W. H. Gilroy, Richard's Landing, St. Joseph Island, 14 Bruce county, Ont.
C. Vanhorn, " " 5 Collingwood.
Wm. Miller, " " 14 Bruce county.
Geo. Miller, " | " 14 "
Robert Miller, " " 14 "
George Hadden, " " 13 Guelph.
John Fyfe, " " 12 "
Amos Cheer, " " 9 Keppal.
Wm. Canfield, " " 12 Ottawa.
Thomas Canfield " " 13 "
Peter Fields, Jr., " " 15 Kent.
Peter Fields, Sr., " " 15 "
W. D. Crowder, Marksville, St. Joseph, 12, Northumberland, Ontario.
Fred. Gray, Carterton, 4, Oxford, Ont.
A. McMaster, Jocelyn, York.
John Wright, Carterton 10.
Joseph Fanson, Marksville, 7 Lambton, Ontario.
Andrew Vincent, " 9, Huron.
Esau Stubbs, " 11, Wellington.
D. McPhail, " 14, "
William Rose, " 13, York.
Thomas Steinberg, " 10, Carleton.
R. Fisher, " 30.
H. Bookman, " 13.
Joseph Hyland, " 13, Wellington.
William Dunn, " 5, "
J. B. Shipman, " 12, "
Thomas Bishop, " 27.
Isaac Wilkins, " 14, Elgin.
R. Turin, " 5.
S. H. Ferris, Jocelyn, 10 years.

Albert Grexton, Jocelyn, 15.

F. H. Court, Richard's Landing, 14 years.

H. Young, Jocelyn, 8 years.

F. H. Young, Jocelyn, 10 years.
R. F. Young, " 5
W. W. Kent, " 10
T. E. Kent, " 5
F. Richardson, " 10
William Henry, Jocelyn 11 years, Durham.
J. C. Reesor, (Reeve) Jocelyn, 8 years, Markham.
Charles Fish, Carterton, 13 years, Northumberland.

Charles Warren, Rose township, (Rydal Bank P. O.) 10 years, Bruce.

Henry Adcock, Tenby Bay (St. Joseph) 13, Warwickshire (Eng.)

John Donaghue, Richard's Landing, 5 years, Hastings, Ontario.

Thomas Canfield, Richard's Landing, 13 years, Ottawa.

S. Flack. Richard's Landing, 12 years, came from Cartwright.

Geo. Hardiman, Tarentorus, (Sault Ste. Marie P. O.) 12 years, Norf lk, Eng.

W. J. Grexton, Richard's Landing, 15 years, Simcoe county.

James Burnside, Seagull, 12 years, Hastings.

John Madden, Seagull, 15 years.

R. Kernaghan, Richard's Landing, 13 years, North York, Ont.

J. J. Marshall, Seagull, 14 years, Huron county, Ont.

George Brander, Seagull, 10 years, Wellington county.

John McGugan, Richard's Landing.

A. McGugan, Richard's Landing.

C. Young, Jocelyn, 14 years.

John Marks, Marksville, 44 years.

A. Vincent,	"	10 years, Middlesex.
J. Fanson.	"	6 years, "
Alex. Scott.	"	20 years, Grey.
A. Hearken.	"	14 " Ottawa.
Jas. Cummings,	"	11 " Wellington.
Thos. Harkens.	"	15 " Bruce.
William Irwin,	"	12 " St. Helens.
Joseph Stewart,	"	5 " Lambton.
R. Chester,	"	12 " Waterloo.
John Biggar,	"	11 " Waterloo.

A. J. McPhee, Marksville, 5 Huron.

W. E. Whyburn, Marksville, 14, Lambton.

D. McArthur, Marksville, 5, Bruce.

John Campbell, Marksville, 8, Waterloo.

Isaac Wilkins, Marksville, 14, Kent.

Wm. Barton, Jocelyn, 12, West Durham.

John Pretty, Seagull, 12, Port Sarnia.

Alex. Gray, Marksville, 14, Elgin county.

Wm. Dunn,	"	4, Waterloo county.
C. Still	"	14, Middlesex.
R. Irwin,	"	5, Wellington.
Fred. Eddy,	"	14, Oxford.
O. See,	"	12, Frontenac.

A. Richardson, Jocelyn.

A. Rains, Seagull.

P. R. Rains, Seagull.

O. T. Rains, Seagull, 40.

Joseph Mitchell, Richard's Landing.

Alex. Ross, Seagull, 14.

Walter Rains, Seagull.

We wish we had space to publish the interesting remarks occuring all along opposite the names, and written in the signer's own handwriting such as:

"It is a good country for farmers."

"Good place for root crops and grain; also very good market."

"Consider it a good place to raise stock and grain and roots and a good market."

"Good for roots, apples, grain, hay, stock and one of the best markets in Ontario."

"Good country for grain and root crop."

"Well adapted for stock."

"Climate particularly adapted for stock."

Talk about evidence! Does the reader want better evidence as to the great inducements and opportunities Algoma offers to the settler seeking a new home?

Can the Governments of Ontario or of Canada demand better or stronger evidence than we have published in above columns to prove that it is their bounden duty to come in and assist us in our immigration and colonization work as they are asked to do by all the Public and Representative bodies in this great District?

The reader will notice that the signers of "Algoma Farmers Testify" hail from all parts of lower Ontario and Quebec, and some from England and Michigan. Several of them are prominent men in their own localities; reeves, councillors, school trustees, etc. Will we be told in the future after the publication of this "Algoma Farmers Testify," as we have been in the past, that Algoma is "no good as a farming country,"—that it is not a desirable field of immigration or colonization?

The Ex. committee have also received valuable and interesting letters and communications from the following gentlemen which we trust to be able to publish in some future pamphlet, and in the meantime copies of them may be had free on application to our secretary at Sault Ste. Marie:

Fred West, township Plummer, Rydal Bank P. O., formerly from Lambton Co.; 12 years resident in Algoma.

Jas. D. Ainslie, Reeve of township Burpee; 14 years resident in Algoma. formerly of Roxborough Co., Scotland, and several years engaged in sheep raising in Australia. We will be glad to send free a copy of this letter to any one in England or elsewhere, who wishes to know how favorably Algoma, either the main land or the islands, compares with Australia, New Zealand, and other countries, for sheep raising. Mr. Ainslie says: "I understand sheep raising, have followed it all my life, was engaged in sheep raising in Scotland and afterwards in Australia. In Australia there are the following disadvantages" and he enumerates them.

Geo. Aberdeen, township Korah, Sault Ste. Marie P. O. (a township councillor) 12 years in Algoma, came from Wellington Co., Ont.

Joseph Gamey, township Campbell, Long Bay P. O. 13 years in Algoma.

Mrs. B. Stickley, township Tarbut, Maclennan P. O. came from the Midland counties, England.

Geo. Hardiman, Dairyman, township Tarentorus. Sault Ste. Marie P. O. 12 years in Algoma; came from county Norfolk, England.

Chas. Warren, Rose township, Rydal Bank P. O. 10 years in Algoma. Came from county Bruce.

T. Fanson, Carterton, 6 years in Algoma.

Alex. Gray, Carterton, came from county Elgin.

S. Bishop, Richards Landing, 12 years in Algoma.

Robt. Fanel, Marksville, 13 years in Algoma.

A. McMaster, Marksville, 10 years in Algoma.

Richard Prout, Tenby Bay, 13 years in Algoma.

Thos. Bishop, Marksville.

W. G. Crowder, Marksville.

F. Gray, Carterton.

A. McAuley, Goulais Bay P. O., been in Goulais Bay settlement 8 years. Was on a rented farm in Wellington county and afterwards Simcoe county Ontario.

T. J. McAuley, Goulais Bay P. O. (both of above letters deal fully with the great and many resources of the fertile valleys of the Goulais and Batchewana rivers northwest of the Sault.)

Rev. J. P. MacInnes, (Presbyterian) MacLennan P. O., township Tarbut. (The reverend gentleman's letter ends; "Algoma may be said to be the 'poor man's friend' ". The letter is very interesting and the writer should know whereof he is speaking as his clerical or missionary work takes him over a good deal of the country frequently.

Jno. Dawson president of the Eastern Algoma Electoral Division Agricultural Society.

Wm. Brown, secretary of the same Society. (Write either of the above gentlemen for the prize list etc., of the Fall Exhibition of the Society, to be held at Sault Ste. Marie on the 4th, 5th and 6th of October, 1892, they will be glad to send it to anyone.)

Wm. Harris, J. P. and president of the Day Wells, and Bright Agricultural Society.

W. R. Smyth, merchant, Rydal Bank.

David Currie, miller, Portlock, Tarbut township, and many others.

Do not be afraid to write to us for copies of any of the above letters. Will be glad to mail them to any post office address in the world.

Some weeks ago the Executive Committee issued the following circular through the District:

CIRCULAR No. 6.

DEAR SIR:

May we ask you to try and encourage everyone in your neighborhood to start and write letters descriptive of Algoma and its many inducements as a field of immigration, and colonization, and the home of the intending settler to the various newspapers, magazines, and journals published in the localities from which they come—where they resided at any time in their lives before coming to Algoma? The publishers or proprietors of any newspaper, magazine or journal we are sure will only be too glad to insert any letter or a series of letters descriptive of this great, and growing District of Algoma—"The New Ontario—The New Northwest."

And these letters if written will have a wonderfully good effect in helping "to settle Algoma." We would like nothing better than to see all the different newspapers, magazines and journals published in the different localities in Great Britain, and other places in Europe, and older Canada and some of the U. S. A. from which our settlers, and residents come, contain every day (if daily newspapers) or every week (if weekly journals or newspapers) or every month (if monthly magazines) letters written by people in Algoma descriptive of the land of their adoption. Nearly every man, and woman can with a little thought, and by taking a little time compose, and write a good newspaper letter, and if there are any mistakes in spelling or grammar it does not matter. The newspaper men will correct that. They are used to bad spelling, and bad grammar. They will be only too glad to get the letters, and to correct bad spelling and grammar if necessary.

Don't let anyone hesitate because he or she thinks they can't write a suitable letter. Kindly make this generally known, and try and get every one iu your neighborhood to start at once and write letters or a series of letters as above mentioned.

It will be like "casting bread on the waters." We shall see the result, and the crop some day if we only all "pull together," and work hard, and use every means at our command to try and get Algoma "fair play."

———

The following letters show that the people in the District CAN write letters to the newspapers.

To the "Huron Expositor," Seaforth.

DEAR EXPOSITOR:—As I very seldom see in your paper, or any other paper anything about Algoma, I will send the following, which may be of some interest to you, and perhaps to some of your readers, who inten l going to some new country to try and better their position. In the first place, regarding the size of Algoma, I might say it is by far the larger part of Ontario; with thousands of acres of first-class soil that would support a large population if cleared and properly farmed. I have been up here two years and, during that time I have seen and raised as fine crops of peas and oats as I ever saw grown in Huron, and for roots of all descriptions it cannot be surpassed in any country. The reason that Algoma does not advance more rapidly than it does are as follows: The farmers who came to Algoma were all poor and generally had large families, consequently they could not stay on their farms and improve them, but had to work in the lumber camps to make money to buy flour and other necessaries of life. And the second reason is that the men on the farms, do not depend on their crops, but on the timber, for which they receive good prices, and instead of clearing their land they are in the lumber camps, or are taking out ties, paper wood or logs, and neglect their farms, and until the timber along the lakes and rivers is all taken away Algoma will never be a farming country. But I am certain if men would lay aside lumbering and attend to their farms, they would be in far better circumstances than they are at the present, because, for what they raise they obtain the highest price. Some people run away with the idea that the whole district is a rock-bound, cold country, inhabited by Indians and wild animals. But that is not the case, as the climate here is superior to that of Huron in many respects. It is a little colder, but it is far drier and more healthy, and the summer is not so hot, and there is as much difference between the fall season of here and the fall season of Huron as between day and night, as we never have those wet, foggy days, but always dry and bright and the longer a man is here the better he likes it. I think if a man comes up here with as much money as it takes to start in Dakota, or the northwestern states or countries he could do better, as the would escape the summer frosts and the terrible cold of the Northwest, and grow just as good crops and get much more for them, and in two years he would be better off than in those other countries in ten years. Yours, Etc.,

ANDREW CLARK.

Iron Bridge, Algoma District.

(The above also appeared in the Toronto Daily and Weekly Empire.)

From correspondence to the "Algoma Pioneer."

DAY MILLS.

There is a farmer, Mr. W. Broch, in the township of Parkinson, who moved in there three years ago without one dollar. He now informs me that he has 40 acres cleared, and the last year, 1891, he raised one hundred bushels of good wheat, a good crop of oats and peas, 600 bushels of turnips, and 350 bushels of potatoes; he has ten head of cattle and one horse all paid for; and out of debt. His boys earning this winter $20 a month in the lumber shanty, and they intend to chop and clear a large fallow this coming summer. He says it is all nonsense about not being able to raise wheat in Algoma. He advises the farmers to work and be industrious and they will be able to tell the same story he does. I might mention that this farmer brought a load of good fall wheat to the mill, and there is no doubt but he will eat good bread from the same wheat.   ALGOMA.

From correspondence to the "Algoma Advocate."

SOWERBY NEWS.

Fine growing weather.

Farmers are all done seeding.

Trout fishing is good, and some of our local sports have been hauling them in by the bag full.

Land hunters are already coming in thick and fast and any person wishing to secure a good home or make a profitable investment could not do better than locate in this part of Algoma, where we have abundance of the purest water—the finest climate in Ontario—the best grass country in the world. Timothy and clover now (the 29th of May) measuring from eight to ten inches in height. Where we can grow root crops and vegetables unequalled in any other part of Ontario, and where wheat, oats and peas grow in abundance. Where the farmer has abundance of timber for fuel and where he can manufacture his own syrup, sugar, vinegar and soap. Where you can travel any and every day in the year without encountering a cyclone or blizzard, and where summer frosts never destroy the fruits of the farmer's labor.

Gus.

The following letters appeared in recent issues of the Toronto Globe and give a brief description of the splendid farming lands to be found in the District :—

Editor Globe.—It is strange that so little is known about the District of Algoma, and the little that is known speaks of mountains and broken country. This is partly true, but there are townships and valleys between the mountains of the best land for agricultural purposes, equal to the best land in Ontario. For instance, when one makes a voyage on one of the steamers from any port on Lake Huron to Port Finlay, Algoma, and travels the Government roads through the townships of Tarbut and Laird, he will pass through a fine country, farms on both sides of the road, near stores, churches and schools. The land bears heavy crops in both sorts of wheat, peas, oats and barley when properly worked, as the soil is a heavy clay, but when once broken the work of ploughing is easier with every year. At present there are no thistles, wild oats or obnoxious weeds in the land, and a careful farmer will take care to keep the land clean. The climate is very healthy and in some respects superior to any other part of Ontario ; there are no disastrous storms, no drought, no wet season (I speak from twelve years experience), and there is the best of drinking water. People who can command from $800 to $3,000 can buy second hand farms from 80 to 240 acres, with clearings from 20 to 60 acres. Taking out wood, ties and saw logs is the winter work, as there is a great demand and every farmer is busy and earns from $200 to $500. Anyone who intends to come here to buy a farm should come in the spring, or later, and look for himself. The cost from any port east of Lake Huron to Port Finlay by steamer is about $5, and if he will come to my place, I am ready to give information as far as I can.

Chas. Venn.

Laird Township.

Editor Globe.—I quite agree with Mr. Venn's account, in his letter in the daily Globe of 26th inst., of the lands in portions of Algoma for agricultural purposes. As seen from the deck of a steamer, the whole coast line of the north shore of the Georgian Bay to the head of Lake George is very rocky and leads to the conclusion that the whole country is of a similar character.. Yet there are, a short distance back from the shore, large stretches of good agricultural lands extending from Blind River (and quite likely east of that point also) all along the north shore to Sault Ste. Marie. About a mile back from Port Finlay, there are new farms of as rich, loamy soil and as easily cultivated as are to be found in the best sections of Ontario. Easy access is had to these lands by the Government roads, and also by the C. P. Railway (Sault Branch), which has stations at easy distances. In some localities, the timber is principally spruce, balsam and mixed maple and other woods and all of it is now valuable for fibre, pulp and other economic purposes. In three or five years after clearing the land, nearly all of the stumps can be easily removed, leaving the land as free of stumps as any farm in other portions of Ontario that has taken, at least, ten years to get into that condition. In some localities. the soil may be a heavy clay, as Mr. Venn states, but in the township of Tarbut, Tarbut additional, a part of Laird and, I believe, in Johnstan and other townships, the soil is loamy, rich, easily cultivated and drained. I am greatly surprised that so many farmers go to the Northwest when such good lands so near at hand and easily reached can be had at a very cheap rate, and that can be made into excellent farms and homes in so short a time.

JOSHUA ADAMS,

Sarnia.

PRINCE, DENNIS AND PENNEFATHER TOWNSHIPS.

This section is beautifully situated on the South shore of Goulais Bay, is heavily timbered and well watered. Hard wood such as birch and maple are especially plentiful and afford excellent advantages in the cordwood trade as the shipping can be all done by water. Pulp wood is also abundant, quite a trade being carried on in that line already; this part of Algoma is well adapted for stock raising, especially sheep and cattle for which we always have a ready market, and for growing timothy and clover, and roots of all kinds the country is unsurpassed. Grain of all kinds does well here, both spring and fall wheat have been grown and is a sure crop but owing to the want of a grist mill no quantity has ever been raised, but now that the

Water Power canal at the "Sault" will soon be completed and mills erected thereon, we hope that difficulty will be removed and wheat be grown in abundance. Fruit can be grown successfully, apples crab-apples and all kinds of small fruits, black-currants and tame strawberries do especially well, and in its season we have a plentiful supply of wild fruit, such as raspberries, huckleberries, etc.

Summer frosts in this locality are unknown. Our market which is the Sault is a good one, as we always get ready sale and good prices for any produce we may take in. As a rule, butter averages 20 cents the year round; never below 17 cents in the summer. Potatoes run at 50 cts. per bushel and oats 50 cents per bushel.

We are situated about thirteen miles from town, and have a government road out of the settlement to the main roads leading to the Sault, and we expect to have a school house erected about the centre of the settlement not later than November of this year, and in conclusion we would say to any wishing to make themselves a home, that there are a great many advantages here over other new countries, and that with small means they would find it hard to better themselves. It is our opinion that anyone coming here with a knowledge of farming, willing hands and about $200. in cash or less, can do well on any of the many free grants to be got, of course those coming with more, could do still better.

Any person or persons desirous of obtaining any further information, will be gladly communicated with by applying to the undersigned.

> AMOS HUGHES, Prince Township.
> MALCOME ALLEN, "
> JOS. THOMPSON, "
> HENRY ROGERSON, Dennis Township.

Sault Ste. Marie, P. O. Ont. Box 113.

☞ We are just advised by The North Shore Navigation Company (Limited) that they will issue tourists and land explorers' tickets, good to stop over at all the ports on the North Shore or the Islands of Manitoulin, Cockburn or St. Joseph, for thirty days or longer if necessary. They also promise to give cheap passenger and freight transportation to settlers moving into the District. They assure us of their hearty sympathy and co-operation in every way possible. Their steamers sail from the ports of Collingwood, Meaford, Owen Sound, and Wiarton. For full particulars and folders call on or write their president, M. Burton, Barrie; their general manager W. J. Sheppard, Waubaushene; or their secretary treasurer C. E. Stephens, Collingwood.

The C. P. R. Company have also promised tourist and land explorers tickets at reduced rates and cheap passenger and freight transportation to settlers moving into the District from any point in Ontario or Quebec to any point in Algoma either on the Main Line or the Soo Line.

If this circular reaches you in time do not forget to send a reporter or special correspondent from your journal to attend the Annual Picnic of the Eastern Algoma Farmers' Institute, to be held in Grove at Thessalon, on the (11th) Eleventh August instant. It is expected to be the largest gathering of farmers and others ever held in the District. A good many prominent gentlemen in the District are advertised to speak on this occasion, besides Jas. Mills, Esq., M.A., the President of the

Agricultural College at Guelph. Amongst other speakers and subjects we note the following on the posters: A. B. Dunn, of Dunn's Valley; Wm. Harris, Day Mills; Mayor Barrett, Thessalon; H. Feltham, Thessalon: "Does Farming Pay " R. A. Lyon, Soo: "Algoma, Its Past;" A, G. Duncan, Soo : "Algoma, Its Future;" Fred. Rogers, Soo; "Loyalty to Algoma;" Wm. Brown, Soo; "The Benefits to be Derived by Farmers from Agricultural Societies and Farmers' Institutes." D. Bole, Soo ; "Algoma as a Desirable Field for Immigration and Colonization."

The North Shore Navigation Co. (Ld.) will give you a very cheap special excursion rate to attend this picnic. Their comfortable and well appointed steamers sail from the ports of Collingwood, Meaford, Owen Sound and Wiarton, and you can reach their steamer at the port most convenient to you. We are sure you will find true hospitality on the City of Midland and the City of Lon lon at all times, or at the same time they will give you the tourist ticket mentioned. Their steamers sail up the St. Mary river from Thessalon to Sault Ste. Marie and call at *all* the ports in the district, and you should run up to the District town either by rail or boat when you are at Thessalon. The C. P. R. Co. will also give you an Algoma tourist ticket if you write, A. B. McNicoll, General Passenger Agent, Montreal, or L. O. Armstrong, Colonization Agent C. P. R., Montreal. Both the latter company and the North Shore Navigation Co. are also preparing to issue cheap excursion tickets from any point in Ontario and Quebec to Sault Ste. Marie for the last two weeks in September and the first two weeks in October, during which the different Fall Fairs will be held throughout Algoma. The Annual Exhibition of the District Agricultural Society will be held at the town of Sault Ste. Marie on the 4th, 5th and 6th days of October. The Society have good grounds and buildings. Every year this Exhibition is becoming more of an "event." It was attended last year and the year before by hundreds of people from all over the State of Michigan and from the lower parts of Ontario and Quebec. The exhibits shown at the last two Fairs in all lines of grain, roots, cattle and sheep could not be equalled anywhere, and this year the Directors expect the Exhibition will eclipse anything before attempted, as "the Colonization and Immigration movement in Algoma" has given an impetus to the farming community all over the District. If you think anything written by the Actual Settlers in this pamphlet is overdrawn, come up and see this Exhibition for yourself, and bring your wife and children with you, or send a reporter or correspondent. There is the best Hotel accommodation now at the Sault. Write the President or Secretary of the Eastern Algoma District Agricultural Society for Prize List and Rules and Regulations. Write the above Railway or Steamship officials for cheap rates to the Soo during the Fair time. By taking a few days before and after the District Fair you could at the same time have an opportunity to visit the one-day Exhibitions of the different Branch or Township Agricultural Societies throughout the District, amongst others Laird Township at Bar River, Bruce Mines, Thessalon, Marksville, Richards' Landing, and a good many others throughout the entire District. You could see some or all of them as well as the larger one of the District or Parent Society at the Sault. The Secretary of the District Agricultural Society will write you the names and dates of the Branch Township Societies if you drop him a post card asking him for the information.

GOULAIS AND BATCHEWANA SETTLEMENTS.

To the Editor of the EXPRESS:

The settlement commonly known as the Goulais Bay settlement, consists of the townships of Vankoughnet, Fenwick and Haviland; all partially settled. Large quantities of excellent lands however remain to be settled at the very low price of fifty cents per acre.

The first settler located in this settlement some eight or nine years ago, and we have now upwards of two hundred inhabitants, all prosperous and happy with no fear of destructive western blizzards and cyclones. We have as fine soil as can be found anywhere in the world, in fact an emigrant can find any soil he may desire from a rich sandy loam to a heavy clay.

The above named townships are well watered by the Goulais River flowing in a westerly direction through the townships and emptying into Lake Superior about twenty-five miles from Sault Ste. Marie. They are also well watered by the Harmony and Cranberry rivers, and a large number of smaller streams and spring creeks, making an abundant supply of pure water.

We have two schools in the settlement, which at the present, are sufficient for the requirements of the settlers.

As regards taxes, we have only school taxes to pay, which is only a mere trifle in comparison to what we had to pay in the older settled parts of Ontario.

We also have church every Sabbath by Methodist and the Church of England ministers, and Sabbath School also every Sunday afternoon. Regarding marketing of our produce, we have communication twice a week during the summer season with Sault Ste. Marie by steam boat, also by driving to town over the Government road a distance of twenty miles where we have an excellent market, which I believe can not be equalled in Ontario, as the following prices for a few of our products will show viz: Butter 18 to 25 cents per pound. Eggs 15 to 20 cents per dozen. Potatoes 40 to 60 cents per bushel, oats 45 to 55 cents per bushel, and other products accordingly. I might here say that the above are not the extreme prices but the average price the whole summer through.

A reader of the above may think that with such excellent lands and fine crops and good prices, that there is something the matter, or we would have a larger population in the time that has elapsed since the first settler located here. To all such I would say, that there has been something wrong for a few years, namely, neglect on the part of the Dominion and Ontario Governments in building a decent road to Sault Ste. Marie, and also in advertising Algoma lands as farming and grazing lands but expending large quantities of money in advertising Manitoba and Northwest lands. But I am happy to say that the Governments have at last awakened to their duty, and have built us a magnificent bridge over the Goulais River, and are at present repairing our road, so

I expect by the end of the year, we will have a road that will compare favorably with any in the District. I might say that anyone desirous of obtaining further information or of seeing for themselves will be gladly assisted by myself and others on application.

I remain, yours truly,
THOMAS A. McCAULEY,

Goulais Bay, Algoma.

PENNEFATHER TOWNSHIP.

To The Editor of The Express.

DEAR SIR;—I was glad to see the letter in your valuable paper last week about Prince, Dennis and Pennefather Townships.

I have travelled over a good many of the United States both West, South and Northwest and I have not seen a better country for general farming purposes than Algoma; as to its capabilities in dairying and cattle raising I can truthfully say this, it cannot be beat anywhere, I have been all through noted cattle ranching countries such as southern Colorado, Texas, Arizona, Montana and other States: the last three are very noted cattle raising countries and in my opinion Algoma excels them all for the following reasons: The abundance of all kinds of grasses and clover, their rapid growth. The white clover is natural to the soil in Algoma and is always a sure crop. In the countries I mentioned, clover does not grow at all.

Roots are also a sure crop in Algoma, never known to fail. The grass crop in Algoma in my opinion may be truthfully said always to be a sure crop. This year I expect to have two tons of hay to the acre, and my oat crop 40 bushels to the acre, and my peas 20 to the acre.

The abundance of water: there is good spring water everywhere in Algoma. Living springs and creeks wherever you go. Good water is half the battle in cattle raising. If the reader were living in the States I have mentioned he would know what I mean. The water over all the prairie and plain states is alkali, brackish water, muddy dirty water. If you want to appreciate good water go there and then return to Algoma. As to markets, our markets are far better than any place I know of East, West or South and I have travelled considerably. I came here from the States to Algoma about three years ago and I like it very well and I have talked with settlers all over this country and have compared notes with them.

As to hog raising: It will pay here very well. You can sell your young pigs from 5 to 6 weeks old at $5 to $6 a pair right here in my own Township, and we have a good market for pork at Sault Ste. Marie all the year round. A better market than they have in Toronto. Hogs are easily raised here, live on clover, and a little chop and one thing and another. My brood sow and pigs run out all summer in the pasture. I sold 18 young pigs this spring at $5 a pair and it paid me very well. I raised them from two sows, I am going to keep at that business.

Poultry pays well here, eggs running from 16c to 35 cents a dozen. They are 16c now (July 23) and in winter up to 35 cents. And as to sheep, the fact of the white clover being here and the excellent water settles that.

I live in West Korah, there is no Free Grant or 20 cents an acre land left in that township, but there is a township north of me called Pennefather, containing excellent land and open for settlement. There are no settlers at present in the township of Pennefather and there is room in it for any amount of people, the land is Indian land open for location and settlement. By going there farmers would only be from 8 to 14 miles from Sault Ste Marie, good Government road.

I know the land well in the township of Pennefather, have travelled over a great deal of it. It is a rolling country, splendid hardwood, good deep, rich, soil. In some places, that is along the route of Goulais Bay road, there are ridges of stone and this deceives a person because there might be a bluff of ten acres of stone on a man's place and one looking at it might think it was stone all over the man's farm on account of the timber being thick and not being able to see any distance, when as a matter of fact the rest of the farm, 150 acres might not have a single stone on it. It is this way all over the North Shore, the rock is altogether in "bluffs" or "ridges," the rest of the land pretty free from stone, sometimes there are boulders which can be easily removed.

The Goulais Bay road at present is the only road running from the Sault into Pennefather township until the town line between Korah and Pennefather is opened. The Goulais Bay road is built along the bluff or ridge of rock all the way through and to travel on it it gives a person a wrong impression of the country. In driving to Goulais Bay from the Sault one would think it a very rough country but a few yards back on either side of the road the bluff ceases and there is good rich soil and free of stone. But even the rocky bluff makes excellent pasture land, the white clover grows there naturally and the broken land on a man's farm in Algoma is always valuable for pasture.

The settlement of the township of Pennefather has been delayed owing to its rough appearance from the road. If people want to see what the township is they must leave the Goulais Bay road and not judge by the land on each side of it as it is built along the rocky ridge or bluff all the way from West Korah to the height of land. To see the township of Pennefather one should go up the Town Line by Hodge's and Allard's farm they lie near the town line of Korah and Pennefather; as I said there is room in the township for any amount of settlers and I will be glad to give any information in my power about it if anyone will call on me at my farm in West Korah or write me to Sault Ste. Marie post office. I won't think it any trouble. They might also write to or call on Wm. Allard, West Korah.   CHARLES ROONEY.

July 23rd 1892.

In connection with what Mr. Rooney says about the broken and rough appearance of Algoma we would call attention to the remarks made editorially in this paper of a recent date on the "Progress of the District."

We then said "and there is not a hundred acres that is not watered by living streams, *nor is there a settler's farm that' is not benefitted to the extent of at least one hundred dollars per year, by having the broken land lying near for pasturage.* Increased attention is being paid to cattle and sheep, and a splendid market for lambs is found at Buffalo, while Toronto buyers appreciate the Algoma cattle."

I have much pleasure in corroborating Mr. Rooney's above statements which I have just read in my paper. I came from Kent, England, near Maidstone. I will be glad to answer any letters about Pennefather or the neighborhood. I hope people in Kent, England, will write me. This is a good country and I advise English tenant farmers to come and buy land and settle in Algoma and not go out on the bleak prairies and plains where they won't find good water or wood. I live on the town line of Korah and Pennefather ; I was the first settler in Korah : I had to cut the road when I went in, 16 years ago, and carry flour on my back and suffer hardship. Now everything is different—good roads and a large town 9 or 10 miles off.

(Signed.)　　　HORACE HODGE,
Sault Ste. Marie P.O., or Korah P.O., Algoma.

We earnestly beg of the settlers all over this great Electoral District to comply with the request contained in circular No. 6. The newspapers of Great Britain and America, we are sure, will only be too glad to publish letters and statements from actual settlers, giving facts and figures about "Algoma, the New Ontario, the New Northwest."

Statistics as to the markets in Algoma.

AGRICULTURAL IMPORTS.

(From the SAULT EXPRESS, August 15, 1891.)

The report of the committee composed of Sheriff Carney, J. Dawson and Councillor Londry to enquire into the quantity of agricultural produce imported to town per annum is astounding. There is no reason that all of the following should not be grown in the vicinity of the town.

IMPORTS.—Wheat, 912 bushels; oats, 17,636 bushels; barley, 800 bushels; peas, 420 bushels; chopped feed, 117 tons; flour, 3,661 barrels; potatoes, 6,272 bushels; butter, 52,429 pounds; eggs, 29,168 dozens; cheese, 9,876 pounds; honey, 2,000 pounds; bacon, 5,355 pounds; fat cattle, 1,029 head; sheep, 714 head; pigs, 651 head; lard, 16,655 pounds; dressed poultry, 2 tons.

From the showing of the forgoing figures we deplore the fact that the sparcity of farmers to cultivate the rich virgin soil of Algoma is the main cause that such arge quantities as shown in the foregoing list have to be imported, when if there were more farmers and the large tracts of land were cleared and cultivated, every article of the enumerated list could be produced and raised in quantity and quality equal to most parts of Ontario, we speak from actual experience as to some, and from observation, having resided in Sault Ste. Marie and vicinity for 16, 19 and 25 years respectively. The average yield per acre being for wheat, 28 bushels; barley, 30 bushels; oats, 40 bushels; peas, 30 bushels, potatoes, 300 bushels; hay 1½ tons. This, considering new land, a portion of the area being still uncleared from stumps. is a good showing. The average price for wheat being $1.00 per bushel; barley, 75 cents; oats, 55 cents; peas 80 cents; potatoes, 50 cents, and hay $12 per ton. Good arable land partly cultivated and bush lands within a radius of four miles of the town of Sault Ste. Marie can be purchased from $4 to $20 per acre, and of a radius of from 4 to 10 miles of the town from $1 to $10 per acre. The climate of Algoma has often been thoroughly misunderstood, not by its residents, but by those unfamiliar with its conditions and misrepresentations made abroad by persons who had more interest in soliciting aid than the welfare and progress of the district. Coupled with the remarkable healthfulness of the district is the fact that it is a most productive country caused by a fortunate combination of soil, temperature and moisture. During the growing season the long sunny days coupled with the cool nights and heavy dews, which are often as good as a shower of rain, give the right conditions to produce abundant yield and bring vegetation to a rapid development. The country is particularly adapted for dairying and for stock raising, the yield of grass being beyond all comparison and truthfully the same can be said of all kinds of root crops. In conclusion, Algoma offers every advantage for profitable farming with climate, soil and pure water, which makes it one of the most productive districts suitable for settlement on the continent of America. These are facts that cannot be refuted.

IMPORTS INTO SAULT STE. MARIE YEARLY.

Statement of Mr. J. H. Meir, Merchant, Sault Ste. Marie, formerly of Owen Sound:

FRED. ROGERS, ESQ., Secretary Algoma Land & Colonization Company.

DEAR SIR,—In answer to your request to give my views and experience as a dealer in produce for some time in this district, I will do so as briefly as possible. For five seasons I have imported on an average over 4,000 dozen eggs and 50,000 pounds butter, besides large quantities of grain and vegetables, such as can be and are profitably grown in the district. Last year I paid one lower lake port firm over $3,000 00 for produce. There are at least a half dozen dealers here who import just as freely one or two probably treble or quadruple as much as myself. Not one dollar of this large amount should ever leave the district, as the supplies for which it goes out could all be successfully produced at home. As to prices, my experience is this : Up to this season I have never known potatoes to sell under forty cents per bushel, and even at that figure for a comparatively short time in the fall only. I think I would be safe in stating that 75 cents has been below rather than above the average price paid for the past five years. Farmers here during this time have never received less than 18 cents per pound, for butter and the same per dozen for eggs. It is a well known fact that some make an all year-round contract for butter and eggs at 25 cents, respectively. Oats are imported to the extent of thousands of bushels, rarely bringing less than 50 cents. Scores of tons of pressed hay find a good market, never ranging under $12 per ton, oftener bringing $14 and $16. Other grains, corn, peas, barley, etc., principally in the shape of chop, come in also in large quantities and are readily sold at correspondingly high figures. Probably 15,000 bags of flour are annually sold here, but under present conditions, and probably for many years to come, farmers anywhere in Ontario will find it more profitable to buy and confine their attention to the growing of other cereals than wheat. Those who cultivate small fruits, particularly strawberries, find a ready market at very high prices. Only last week I saw primo fruit selling in Toronto at five cents per small basket. On my return trip I purchased a lot at Richard's Landing, in Algoma, for which I paid 12 cents for the same sized basket—a price which is steadily maintained all through the season. I know of no place better adapted for the successful raising of small fruits than this vicinity, or where any such high prices can be obtained. From what I have seen of this part of the District of Algoma, I confidently believe there are advantages for the thrifty and enlightened farmer that no other part of our fair Province possesses, much less that of the neighboring States, where so many of our population have gone. It may be said that if the thousands of acres of good land lying idle and unproductive around us were brought under cultivation, the present high prices of produce would cease. Further, it might also be reasonable to suppose that we would become exporters instead of importers, and that our distance from outside markets would depreciate values very much. To these objections I would answer that such a result is highly improbable. It is only a question of time until the vast and almost unlimited resources of this district, in minerals, etc., will be developed a thousand fold and the present good home market of our settlers will, in consequence, not only be continued, but materially improved in every respect.

Wishing your Company every success in your laudable enterprise of endeavoring to attract settlers to this highly favored portion of our Province, as well as striving to keep the " Canadians for Canada."

I am, yours, etc.,
J. H. MEIR.

Mr. W. WILLIAMSON, of Jocelyn, just writes us :

" As to early crops, I have been using new potatoes daily since the 15th of July. Frequently other years I have had them by the 4th of July. I have been using cucumbers, peas, beans, vegetable marrows, and other garden things right along for the past ten days or so. These were not forced, but grown in the open air without any extra trouble. I grow any amount of tomatoes, sweet corn and other things only supposed to grow in warm climates, and my neighbors raise any amount of fruit, apples, plums, cherries, crab apples, strawberries, black, red and white currants, etc.

As to prices: I sold new potatoes yesterday (August 2nd,) for $1 per bushel; small cucumbers, 40 cents per doz.; butter beans and peas, 30 cents per pail."

MARKET GARDENING, DAIRYING AND SMALL FARMING.

One point not touched on in the letter of Mr. Meir, and the report of Messrs. Dawson, Carney and Londry, is the effect the opening of the Canadian ship canal at the Soo, will have on the question of markets in Algoma.

The passenger traffic through the Canadian canal will be immense. We clip the following from a recent newspaper. If the figures are incorrect they can easily be corrected.

"During the year ending June 30 last Canadian steamers carried 12,973 passengers through the Sault canal. American steamboats carried 13,317 passengers."

All this traffic goes now through the American canal; none of it comes to the Canadian side. When our canal is finished, the Canadian Soo will get the benefit of the Canadian passenger and freight business. The freight traffic is something immense; and both the freight and passenger traffic is yearly increasing. We have frequently read that the tonnage of the vessels passing through the present locks on the American side of the river, during the 8 or 9 months of the year during which the canal is open yearly, far exceeds the traffic which passes through the famous Suez canal in the whole 12 months. This statement may give some idea of the great commerce already existing between the towns and cities, states and provinces bordering on that great inland sea, Lake Superior, and the rest of the world, and this commerce is yearly increasing. The American government is also building a second canal on their side of the river, and marine men think inside of the next five or ten years if the traffic keeps on yearly increasing, even the three canals can hardly handle the marine business at the two Soos. Furthermore, there is a strong agitation on foot in both countries to induce the governments of Canada and the United States, to deepen our waterways to a uniform depth of 20 feet, so as to allow the ocean traffic, instead of stopping at Montreal, to continue on up to Sault Ste. Marie, Port Arthur and Duluth. This is almost certain to be done within the next few years. During the time when the Bruce Mines copper mines were running sailing vessels made several trips from Bruce Mines to Swansea, (Wales,) and a "whaleback" steamer recently made the through trip between West Superior City or Duluth and Liverpool. Marine men on the great lakes confidently expect that Sault Ste. Marie, Port Arthur and Duluth, and the other ports in Algoma,

Minnesota and Wisconsin, bordering on the great lakes, will inside of this present decade become practically ocean ports, and that passengers and freight will be able to go directly from those ports to Liverpool, London and other transatlantic ports. Already scores of the passenger and freight steamers, sailing up the St. Mary's river equal in every way the average ocean steamer, and several of them, notably the C. P. R., Lake Superior fleet, are Clyde-built vessels. What does all this mean to the farmer, stock raiser, fruit grower, or market gardner settling now in Algoma? It all effects the great question of supply and demand. Besides the 12,000 passengers carried on British vessels through the American canal during the last 12 months, there were thousands of officers and men belonging to this great merchant marine, both passenger and freight, who had to be fed as well as the passengers. Every large freight steamer or sailing vessel carries a large crew, and then it will be remembered that the 12,000 passengers mentioned does not include the passengers carried by the several fleets of "local" steamers, both Canadian and American, which stop at the Soo and do not go through the canal at all, and therefore were not counted on the canal register. The tonnage, passenger and freight traffic of these local lines is already something immense and is yearly increasing. Several of these local steamers are splendid specimens of marine architicture. What does all this mean to the market gardener and small farmer settling in Algoma? Inside of the next few months it is confidently expected that not only will the great ship canal at the Canadian Soo be nearing completion, but that the greater water power canal at the Canadian Soo will be finished, and immense flour mills, pulp and paper mills, furniture and other factories be in the course of erection on its banks. These two great canals are being built almost side by side. Each of them, a few years ago, would have been looked upon as an almost impossible engineering feat. So also would have been the opinion a few years ago, regarding the great International railway bridge between the twin cities of Sault Ste. Marie which crosses the site of both canals just before it spans the rapids of the Soo river.

But at the latter end of the nineteenth century one should be surprised at nothing. Look at the great "whaleback" steamers and barges passing through the canal. Five years ago their projector and inventor was laughed at. Now they are bidding fair to revolutionize marine ship building. When one looks at the great International Bridge across the rapids and at the large Ship Canal and Water Power Canal now nearing completion, and at the "whalebacks" passing down the river, he or she is not likely to laugh at the assertion confidently made all along the coast that in ten years, at the furthest, the "twin cities of Sault Ste. Marie" will be practically and to all intents and purposes, ocean ports. The question of the deepening a few channels here and there between the Soo and Montreal—and the deepening of the Welland canal—is only one of dollars and cents ; and even if the Canadian Government does not co-operate the American Government will do the work alone. If you doubt this, read the reports and proceedings of the Waterways Commission and read the opinions of the leading American Congressmen on the subject. The deepening of the great inland highway of commerce of the world between Duluth and the seaboard is already a live question in American politics. It is looked upon as a national as well as a commercial necessity, and there are enough " hustlers " in the great marine cities of the great lakes to push the scheme through.

Well, does not all this go to prove conclusively that, good as the markets are already in Algoma, in a few years there will be such a demand for everything which a farmer, stock raiser or fruit grower can raise or grow, that Algoma would need to have a good settler on every 40 acres in the whole Electoral District—in size a Province—in order to be able to supply the home market. If you doubt this, read over again Mr. Meir's letter and the report of Messrs. Dawson, Carney and Londry. Then consider the ship canal question. the water power question, and the timber and mineral industries in Algoma which are only yet in their infancy.

Before leaving the marine question, let us call attention again to the first paragraph of the Petition of the Public and Representative Bodies in Algoma to the Federal and Provincial Governments, printed ante page.

" A settler coming to Algoma can never be at the mercy of railways or of combines." If you do not know what we mean, go and reside in some country at a distance from the Great Lakes and you will find out what we mean, that is if you have any produce to ship or to sell. You will find that the railway carriers, when they have not to meet the competition of steamers and railway vessels, take all, or nearly all, the profit—very little being left for the producer.

The practical remarks made by one of the leading merchants in Algoma at the recent mass meeting held at Thessalon and Iron Bridge, dealt fully with this subject. The subject of his speech practically being: " Who Gets the Profit."

———

Some two years ago Mr. R. A. Lyon, late Member for the District, made the following patriotic remarks on the floor of the Provincial Legislature— they were passed unheeded, politics running high. We now call the attention of the House and the whole world again to them:

It is only in the last few years that the District of Algoma has attracted any special attention, and the idea is just commencing to dawn upon the people of Canada and the United States of the enormous mineral wealth which it contains and the rich agricultural valleys which are to be found within its limits.

*   *   *   *   *

The mineral wealth of Algoma, now that it is beginning to be understood and appreciated, I am confident will be one of the most successful fields for enterprise that we have, not only in Canada, but upon this Continent. In my opinion Sault Ste Marie, in the natural course of things, is bound to become an important manufacturing and shipping centre. The most important factor in the industries of this place will be large smelting works, for smelting purposes.

*   *   *   *   *

I know, Mr. Speaker, there is a disposition on the part of some people to discredit, to a certain extent, the great possibilities of Algoma, but I think that investigation will amply establish the true state of affairs to be that the District of Algoma, which a few years ago was almost unheard of, is one of the most varied and profitable mineral producing regions that the people of any country have been called upon to develop. I entertain no doubt whatever of the mineral productiveness of Algoma, and the ultimate success of the industries which are now being established within the confines of that District. There are people who attach but little importance to such mines as produce the coarser metals, but this view is, certainly, a mistake and a conclusion hastily arrived at, without either proper information or reflection upon the subject. I remember quite well some five or six years ago, when the Lake Superior Gogebic Iron Mining Company, an American institution which operates entirely in Michigan and Wisconsin, were struggling almost for an existence. In the year 1884 they only produced about 1,000 tons of iron ore, but I see that last year, according to reliable mining authority, they produced and shipped to the markets of the world 2,250,000 tons, a marvellous showing when compared with efforts of five years ago. The evidence of careful examination reveals the fact that we have richer mines, and that all that is required to make them a source of financial strength to this country are the facilities and enterprise to bring about their development. Further than the special phase of the question to which I have just alluded, it would be well for the House to carefully consider the value, to this Province, of the large tracts of agricultural lands that will be opened up by the building of the proposed road. I think it of considerable importance to the future welfare of Ontario, that we induce as many of our young men as possible to settle in the new portions of this Province. It is certainly much more desirable than to have them go to the United States, where so many have already taken up homes and settled. The only way to avoid an exodus of this kind is to give some substantial encouragement to the young men to remain in Ontario, and this can only be achieved by opening up for colonization the vast agricultural sections that are to be found in the district which, in part, I have the honor to represent.

*   *   *   *   *

In conclusion, permit me to say that the increased population and the settlement and development of the district have been very rapid within the last few years, but in no section of the district has this been so noticeable as in Sault Ste. Marie. The population four years ago was only 900, and now it is a prosperous town of nearly 4,000. Sault Ste. Marie with all its natural resources and immense water power and situated on the grand highway between the Western States and Territories and the Great Northwest and the sea-board, is destined to become one of the most important manufacturing and shipping cities in the Dominion.

RANDOM NEWSPAPER CLIPPINGS.

Sault EXPRESS July 16th, 1892: While we have had such beautiful weather up here, the nights being so extremely pleasant, while the days are sometimes rather warm, we have during the last two weeks had two letters written on the same day. One from Picton, Ont., to the effect that the weather is cold and wet, and the other from a point near Montreal, that the hot weather there is unbearable both night and day. No wonder that the people like this fine climate.

Strawberries: A farmer in Prince, eleven miles from town, has already marketed over one hundred dollars worth of strawberries at twelve cents per pound, and says he cannot supply the demand even at that figure. Who says the Soo is not a superior market? Last week berries were a drug in Toronto at four and five cents.

Several new settlers have arrived at Richard's Landing, and from various parts of the District, we hear of settlers coming in and taking up lands. We are heartily glad to say that very few of our people are leaving us.

Algoma PIONEER: "Nothing succeeds like success," and this is the root and branch of the agricultural prosperity of Algoma District, where industrious settlers invariably succeed in reaching a position of comfort, and comparative independence, and in less time than in any other part of the Dominion. Experienced farmers, with or without capital, can make money here. And with capital their chances are doubled.

Gore Bay GUIDE, July 16th, 1892: Mrs. Beckerton, of the fourth concession of Gordon, brought in a very fine lot of strawberries in the beginning of this week. A number picked out averaged an ounce in weight.

D. I. Millar effected a sale of about ninety tubs of butter on Monday last for the English market. This speaks well for the quality of Algoma butter. The buyer, Mr. Lloyd, reported himself as well pleased with the quality as a straight lot, and did not cull a single tub. This is the first shipment worthy of note in that direction, and should encourage our farmers. There is no reason why we with our clear running springs, cool nights and abundance of good pasturage should not excel the production of the eastern dairyman.

WHY THE ALGOMA LAND & COLONIZATION CO. WAS ORGANIZED.

At an early stage of "The Immigration and Colonization Movement in Algoma" it was thought by the friends of the movement that we could work to far better advantage and with greater effect as an organized company with a constitution and by-laws and having a board of directors annually elected than we could as an unorganized committee of citizens no matter how popular the movement might be, and therefore the Algoma Land and Colonization Company was founded and organized with the "object to settle Algoma." The first board of directors elected David Gordon, Esq., the President of the Thessalon Agricultural Society, as the first President of the Company, and we think the choice has been satisfactory to the people of the District generally.

THE MINERAL WEALTH OF ALGOMA.

If the items and comments one sees from time to time in the District newspapers are at all to be believed, Algoma possesses greater mineral wealth than any other country in the world; copper, silver, gold, platinum, plumbago, nickel, iron, asbestos and other minerals, apparently are being discovered all along the North Shore. The whole world has read about the deposits of nickel recently found in the townships on the Sault branch and main line C. P. R. around Sudbury, and recently nickel has been found near Thessalon, also gold bearing quartz. We are told minerals of all kinds are found on the Garden River Indian Reserve and in the Batchewana Valley and other places in the District, and iron is being found to the north of and around Echo Lake, and in other places.

We clip the following from recent papers.

Algoma PIONEER: In the days of the settlement of Algoma District, or a quarter of a century back, when thoughtless men called this district "a God forsaken country," it was no easy task to persuade anybody to believe that any good thing could be found therein. And in the palmy days of Bruce Mines, when upwards of 2,000 people were shut up in that one settlement, and it poured its rich copper ores into England, people were disposed to look upon that mine as an oasis in a mighty desert land, rather than as one of a countless number of the richest mineral deposits to be found on this continent. But, as the enterprising pioneer explorers, William Palmer, Joshua Coatsworth, James Stobie and others ventured into the depths of the forest and returned with rich specimens of iron, copper, silver and gold, thoughtful people began to look seriously at its possible mineral resources and to anticipate the day when this despised Algoma District would become as famous for its mines as ever was Cornwall in the Old Land. In the early history of the Pioneer fifteen years ago we frequently alluded to Algoma's destiny as the coming Cornwall of America, and unbelieving people pointed to our granite-bound coasts as proof positive that it was impossible for minerals in any quantity to be discovered here. But, as all things come to him who waits long enough, so the bright day then foreseen by few, has dawned upon Algoma District, and from Rat Portage to Sudbury the district teems with partially developed stores of rich mineral wealth that is beginning to astonish the world. Port Arthur, Silver Islet, Garden River and Sault Ste. Marie, with their deposits of silver, and Desbarret's and Portlock with their iron, Sudbury with its fabulous wealth in copper, nickel and gold, are to-day well established facts that defy contradiction, and assure us of the near approach of the time for the fullest realization of all our hope and aspirations regarding the great and long neglected district. A movement is on foot to throw open the Victoria and other silver mines in this section, and English capitalists have had their attention drawn to the great wealth of nickel lying undeveloped near Sudbury.

Gore Bay Guide : Another very rich find of native gold, in a fine fissure vein, has been discovered in Galbraith, very near the celebrated Ophir mine. The enterprising discoverer, Mr. Mitchell, is deserving all the luck he gets, as he has already spent $30,000 in prospecting in Algoma. He got $16,000 for a nickel mine lately. Messrs. McArthur Bros., a year ago, flatly refused $250,000 cash for the Ophir, and will, they say, never part with it under $300,000.

The best mine, in our opinion, is " Mother Earth," and we advise our settlers to stick to their farming and stock raising and leave " exploring " and " prospecting " to others. There is one thing, however, attractive about the above extracts. If Algoma has all this mineral wealth, and there is no doubt she has a great deal of it, then it ensures good markets for all time to come, because these delvers after hidden wealth must eat and drink and be clothed, and in Algoma, unlike any other country under the sun, mining and agriculture can be carried on almost side by side, and the producer and consumer almost live close together.

THE TIMBER WEALTH OF ALGOMA.

The farmers who come into Algoma are, of course, directly interested in this matter. When they come here they find a valuable crop on their lands already planted by nature and ready to harvest. The timber of all kinds on the farms in Algoma is valuable. A few years ago the soft wood, poplar, balsam, spruce, etc., had no value except for summer firewood ; now it is in great demand as pulp-wood, (paper wood). American firms are buying, all over the district, all the pulpwood they can get and the demand is yearly increasing. It is wonderful how many articles can now be manufactured out of the *papier mache*. We read in the newspapers that not only furniture of all kinds is being made out of it, but car wheels also, and that it is said car wheels so made are preferable to those made out of iron, as they are not affected by the frost. However this may be, it is a fact that the pulp wood industry is an important matter in Algoma and is yearly assuming larger proportions. It is now a well established industry, although only started some two or three seasons ago.

We clip the following from the Sault EXPRESS :

Pulp wood is coming down in great quantities on the Thessalon river; all the wood was hauled to the banks this winter, and the recent rains has helped the drive very much. $100,000 will be spent around Bruce Mines, this summer for pulp wood, and it is expected that business will be very good on the North Shore this summer.

What the Algoma PIONEER says: W. D. Fremlin of St. Joe's Island, is getting out about 8,000 cords of pulp wood this year; Frank Perry and Arthur Crawford about 20,000 cords; Dave Ranson about 8,000 cords; H. J. Myers about 10,000 cords; the Detroit Sulphite Fibre Co., about 12,000 cords; Duncan & Plummer about 5,000 cords; and the Butterfield Lumber Co. about 3,000 cords. In addition to the above there are about 40,000 cords being gotten out by other parties, which makes a total of 106,000 cords, valued on the river bank at about $3.25 per cord, making the actual value of the pulp wood industry to the jobbers in this vicinity $334,500. From the above figures an idea can be had of how much value the pulp wood industry is to the "Soo."

This industry is now wholly in the hands of the Americans, but as our water power canal on the Canadian side of the rapids of the St. Mary's river, at the "Soo," is nearly completed, it is expected that inside of a year or so, Canadian mills at Sault Ste. Marie will be engaged in the manufacture, and that instead of it all going to a foreign country a large part of it will be manufactured as it should be in Canada. There is enough pulp wood in this great District it is believed, to supply the world. Explorations have been made during the last year or two towards the head waters of the Batchewana, Goulais, Garden, Bar, Thessalon, Mississauga and other rivers in the District, and the supply in the back townships lying to the north and west of the town of Sault Ste. Marie, and north of Bruce Mines and Thessalon is said to be inexhaustible.

HARD WOOD FOR CORD WOOD.

There is an active demand and market for hard wood at a good many points in the district. Many of the steamers and tugs (of which the name is legion) plowing the waters of these great inland seas and rivers get their supply of fuel at docks and landing places all along the north shore and the islands. It would be interesting to know the number of cords of hard wood, and perhaps a good deal of soft wood, consumed by the different steamers and tugs and loaded at the different docks and landing places on the north shore between Killarney and Batchewaung Bay, and on the north and south shores of Manitoulin, Cockburn and St. Joseph.

Then the amount of cordwood yearly consumed at "the twin cities of Sault Ste. Marie" is something very large. A large amount is every winter drawn over the ice across the river and sold in the American town. During the season of navigation cordwood is shipped from all over the district to both "Soos" on scows. In summer the market price at the "Soos" is from £4 to $5 (dry) per cord ; in winter about $3 per cord (green.) The other towns and villages also need a yearly supply of cordwood. There is no hard wood now to be had, we are told, within about six miles of the Sault. The hard wood belt beyond that all around the town will, in a few years, be very valuable. Prince, Pennefather and other townships contain excellent hard wood.

MERCHANTABLE HARD WOOD.

Hard wood is rapidly coming into demand throughout older Canada and the States for merchantable use—manufacturing purposes. Once this industry reaches Algoma it will, within a year or two, assume as large proportions as the pine or pulp wood business—perhaps greater. Hard wood, birch and maple, is rapidly coming into demand in older Canada and the States for flooring and the manufacture of furniture, etc. There cannot be found in the world finer maple and birch (and in some parts also excellent oak) than can be found in the hard wood townships of Algoma. In Prince and Pennefather, and we presume in other townships also, beautiful birds-eye maple is found in abundance we believe ; and also we are told in the townships in the valleys of the Batchewaung and Goulais rivers. As soon as the attention of Canadian and American manufacturers is called to the fact that merchantable hard wood so abundantly exists in this great district it will be in active demand for merchantable and manufacturing purposes.

The water power canal now nearly completed, will be a great help in this direction. As farmers all over the District can haul over the snow roads in winter, or ship on scows during the season of navigation, their hard wood logs to the hard wood mills on the canal and have them converted into flooring. Hard wood furniture and cabinet factories will also doubtless be in operation on the canal within a year or two. All this is interesting to the incoming settler in Algoma, because it shows him what value he can expect to receive from the crop of different kinds of timber nature has already planted on his farm, and which is ready to be harvested. Some few weeks ago, a day or two before our recent Gore Bay public meeting, the enterprising agents of some Dakota Railway Co., or "Mortgage Bank Investment Co., we think they called it, mailed to nearly every address in that part of the District some flaming circulars about the State which is the natural home of the blizzard and the grasshopper. One of these circulars had at the top of it a picture representing a field showing some stumps on it, and an owl sitting disconsolately on a saw log, and the picture bore this legend, "one of the disadvantages of farming in a timbered section, no stumps on our farms," (meaning the farms in Dakota of course.) There may be "disadvantages" in connection with farming in a timbered section, but what are the disadvantages?

We have a copy of each of these circulars before us now and we look at them while we write. We happen to notice casually that they do not say anything about the disadvantages of farming in a prairie country. They are silent as to the blizzards in winter, the hurricanes in summer, the hail storms (which save threshing machines), the summer frosts, the dreadful prairie fires, the drouth, the grasshoppers, the brackish alkali water, the absence of springs, the fact that neither timothy or clover will grow there, the want of home markets. The fact that the railway companies are very glad to get a man to emigrate to the home of the blizzard, but that when he gets there he is at the mercy of the railways.

We casually noticed the above omissions. The people of Algoma do not propose to get out illustrated circulars to compete with the Dakota railway or land companies, headed " The Disadvantages of Farming in a Prairie Country,"but we think if we cared to take the trouble we could get out some very effective ones and perhaps thereby get as many Americans to come from the home of the blizzard to Algoma as they hoped by means of their circulars, advertisements and literature, to have got Canadians to leave Canada and go to Dakota. But we do not propose so doing. We simply want to keep " Canada for the Canadians " and the Canadians in Canada.

The literature we circulate through the different States is only addressed to and intended for our fellow-Canadians, who have foolishly left this country, and have not improved their position by so doing.

We are sorry to see in nearly every Canadian newspaper, daily and weekly, flaming advertisements issued by the different American railway and Land companies all over the Union. We are sorry to see their literature flood the land. If their pamphlets, advertisements and circulars told "the truth, the whole truth, and nothing but the truth," we would not object to them at all.

SHEEP RAISING IN ALGOMA.

The reader will notice what the Reeve of Burpee Township says in these pages as to the relative merits of Algoma, Australia and Scotland for sheep raising. If the reader wishes to know further about the disadvantages of Australia in that direction, he could profitably read a very interesting article in Scribners Magazine, (London and N. Y.) for February 1892, entitled "Station Life in Australia," by Sidney Dickinson. He will there read about the drought, the flood, disease among sheep and the heavy mortality, prairie fires or fires on the ranges, the rabbit pest, the locust pest, the absence of spring water, etc., in Australia. Add to all this the great distance sheep have to be driven to the port of shipment, and then that they have to be carried to the other side of the world (their antipodes) to find a market, also the fact that clover will not grow there at all, (while white clover is natural to the soil in Algoma, and the red clover grows anywhere the same as if it were indigenous;) read all that in connection with the evidence contained in these pages and you will think with us that Algoma offers more inducements in the sheep raising business than any other country does or can offer. And remember our markets are close at hand. Big cities within convenient distance for shipment by rail or water wanting all the lambs and sheep we can raise, besides as it is, we cannot supply our home market. If you doubt this write to any one of the firms of butchers at Sault Ste. Marie, Ontario, and ask them if there is a market for sheep and cattle at Sault Ste. Marie, Ontario.

We clip the following articles from the Gore Bay GUIDE :

GREATLY ENCOURAGED.—Many of the settlers in the District were greatly encouraged by their success in raising sheep last summer and are preparing to go into it extensively this year, some intending to keep as many as 100 sheep. The demand for lambs is unlimited, and Algoma cattle have a splendid reputation below. New buyers intend visiting this market, and before long the principal occupation of our farmers will be the raising of cattle. Prices this season promise to be remunerative.

BECOMING FAMOUS.—The soil and climate of Algoma seems to be especially adapted to stock raising. Cattle seem to grow and thrive with wonderful rapidity. This is owing to the healthfulness of the climate ; the abundance of pure water and the rich and nutritious grasses which abound everywhere. Clover seems to be indigenous to the soil of Algoma, and grows everywhere in rich abundance, even on the high rocky lands which are peculiarly adapted for sheep pastures, in fact it seems to be their natural home. Sheep raising has grown with wonderful rapidity in Algoma in the past few years. Our farmers are beginning to find that they do so well and are so profitable that they are rapidly increasing their flocks. Algoma mutton is becoming famous for its excellency and will soon take the lead everywhere. The only trouble is there seems to be danger of its being too fat. There is another point of very great importance, and that is that sheep are not subject to diseases that are found to be troublesome in other parts of the world. In cattle raising, although there has been great improvement in the last two or three years, there is still much room for further development. There are immense areas of the best grazing lands still unoccupied, upon which thousands of cattle might be feeding with large profits to the parties having their money invested. Now, there is one fact in connection with pasture in Algoma that outsiders do not understand, and that is the fact that from the time the snow goes off in the spring until it comes again in the fall the grass and herbage of various kinds are green, fresh and nutritious. It is very rare indeed that the pastures become dried up and worthless as they do in many other parts. It is true that stock of all kinds have to be fed and cared for during the winter, but our climate is not severe ; we are not subject to extremes of either heat or cold. We have no blizzards ; our climate is equable, and therefore not as hard on either man or beast as if we were subject to those sudden variations of temperature. Wheat, oats, peas and other kinds of grain do well in Algoma. Samples of these cereals which have been put in competition against samples from other parts of Ontario, have been found to compare favorably with the best.

PROFITS IN SHEEP RAISING.

We quote the following from an admirable address recently delivered before the Wisconsin State Agricultural Society, by Prof. Craig, of the State University.

Of the numberless sources of profit in breeding sheep, there are three which are much larger and better than the rest. There is a profit to the farm, for it becomes cleaner and more productive. I have noticed that there are but few weeds on sheep farms. A study of the sheep will show that they will eat a greater variety of plants than either cattle, horses or pigs. It has been tried with 500 plants, and it has been found that, when offered, the sheep ate 75 per cent. of them, and the cow and the horse 50 per cent. The power of the sheep to clean farms and live where other farm live stock could not exist is due in a large measure to this.

The farm becomes more productive, for each arable acre becomes richer. If a shepherd will spend 75 cents buying bran for each ewe of his breeding flock, and grow enough clover hay for it, he may sell a fat sheep weighing fifty pounds with its ten pounds of wool, and his farm will increase in fertility. The farm becomes more productive, for every acre is made to yield a profit.

In breeding mutton sheep there is a second profit. It is made on the home-grown foods that are fed to them. Even though the foods that are fed to fattening sheep are charged against them at a good market price, they yet yield a good profit. This is the best kind of a home market. The sheep themselves create the third profit.

The reader of Mr. Dickinson's admirable article in Scribner, will notice that there is lots of money made in the sheep raising business in Australia by those engaged in it; some of those he mentioned are millionaires. But the reader will notice that the only ones engaged in the business there are large range owners. It is like wheat farming on the prairies; to make any money at all, even a living, it has to be carried on on a large scale or not at all. A farmer with small means could no more successfully carry on the sheep business in Australia, than he could the wheat raising business in Dakota.

What our "Algoma Farmers Testify," proves is this: That a farmer, fruit grower, cattle or sheep raiser can come to Algoma with small means, and do very well if he has a fair knowledge of the business he is engaged in, and if he is hardworking.

As the clerical friend we have quoted says: "Algoma is the poor man's friend.' He means that it is the place where a man can come with small means and do well. We want the whole world to know this, and that is why the people all over this great District are petitioning the Provincial and Federal governments to help us in our colonization and immigration work.

FRUIT GROWING.

We have not space to deal with the fruit question. As to the whole fruit question, the reader might correspond with John Dawson, Esq., the President of the East Algoma Electoral Division Agricultural Society. Sault Ste. Marie. As to apples particularly, with Wm. Harris, Day Mills, or with A. Eddy, Marksville ; D. Dunn Jocelyn ; the latter gentleman having a nursery, we think. As to small fruits, Mr. Wm. Sharp, West Korah, who recently read an able paper before the Central Algoma Farmers' Institute on the subject, probably would be willing to give any information in his power.

TO ADVERTISERS.

Our literature will be widely circulated. This and our other pamphlets will be read all over Ontario, Quebec, Maritime Provinces, England, Ireland, Scotland, and a great many, if not all of the United States, and in other countries also.

They thus afford the best possible medium of advertisement.

The Board have been repeatedly urged to allow mercantile advertisements of one kind and another to be inserted in their pamphlets and have been offered large sums for the privilege.

We have hitherto refused all advertisements. However, after further consideration and repeated applications, we have decided to accept in future any advertisement which, in the opinion of the Board, is not foreign to our object—" to settle Algoma."

Any advertisement which may be of public service to the district at large or to the incoming settlers.

We have decided in the future editions of this and our other pamphlets to allow the following advertisements to be inserted at the end of each of our pamphlets, in an advertising supplement :

1. Advertisements of municipal corporations, towns, villages, townships, municipalities, or of semi-municipal corporations, water power companies, boards of trade, etc., calling public attention to the inducements or opportunities offered by any locality in Algoma, either for agricultural, fruit growing or stock raising purposes, or as inviting sites for manufacturers, mills or industrie of any kind, or as summer, health or pleasure resorts at any time of the year.

2. Advertisements of railway companies, either Canadian or foreign, making Algoma their objective point; or selling through tickets to points in Algoma, whether entirely over their own line or partly over their own and partly over some other line of railway or steamship connection.

3. Similar advertisements of steamship companies, either ocean or lake.

4. Advertisements or cards of manufacturers of agricultural implements, etc.

5. Advertisements or cards of nurserymen and seedsmen.

6. Advertisements of improved stock breeders—individuals as well as associations.

7. Such other and similar advertisements as may meet the approval of the Board.

The Board have in preparation the following other pamphlets descriptive of Algoma: "Farming in Algoma," the New Ontario—the New Northwest, with map and views; "Woman in Algoma;" what the farmers' wives and daughters say about "The New Ontario; the New Northwest," being the essays now being written by the farmers' wives and daughters all over Algoma. Mentioned ante page 9.

[The Judges appointed jointly by the Board of the Agricultural Society and the Board of this Company are the following gentlemen: Rev. W. A. Duncan, M.A., B.D.; R. A. Lyon, Esq., ex-M.P.P.; John Dawson, Esq., President East Algoma Agricultural Society. All Essays are to be in the hands of the Secretary of the East Algoma Agricultural Society by the evening of the 24th September. —Ex. Com.]

Subsequent editions of this and our other pamphlets will be issued from time to time, as the company see their way clear to do so. It is only a question of dollars and cents. We firmly believe that the settlement of Algoma is only a matter of dollars and cents judiciously spent in advertising to the world her many inducements and opportunities.

The Minister of the Interior (who has charge of immigration matters in Canada) has kindly offered to send our pamphlets to the High Commissioner and the agents of the Dominion Government on the other side of the Atlantic, to be circulated as they may think best.

This present edition is only 10,000 copies, of which 5,000 will be placed in the hands of the Minister of the Interior, for the above purpose. We are desirous of issuing at the earliest possible moment a second edition of 50,000 copies of this pamphlet, of which 20,000 copies should be for distribution in older Canada, and 30,000 in England, Ireland and Scotland.

We are further desirous of issuing the following foreign editions of this pamphlet.

1. A French edition for circulation in the counties of Essex and Kent, Ontario, from which there has been and is yearly a large "exodus" to the United States, and in the Province of Quebec, and in the New England and other States, to which so many of our French Canadian citizens have gone. We want to turn the "exodus" the other way both as regards our French Canadian absentee citizens, and those of other nationalities.

2. A German edition for circulation in the counties of Perth and Waterloo, Ontario, and in old Germany.

3. A Scandinavian edition for circulation in Norway, Sweden and Denmark.

We are doing what the Governments should do. Algoma "the New Ontario," "the bigger half of Ontario, belongs to Ontario. Should not the Ontario Government help us in our efforts to carry out our "object, to settle Algoma?" Algoma, "the New Northwest" belongs to Canada, should not the Dominion Government help us!

Every reader of these pages can help us in some way or other, if in no other way but by seeing that this pamphlet is not wasted or destroyed, but that it gets into the right hands.

TOURISTS, HEALTH AND PLEASURE SEEKERS.

The District of Algoma should not be forgotten by you when choosing a place for rest or recreation. In summer there is excellent speckled trout fishing in hundreds of creeks and streams; speckled and mountain trout in many an inland lake; black bass, sturgeon, muskilonge, white fish, lake trout, and other fish. Excellent camping grounds, good boating, canoeing and sailing, and you can fetch your wives and children here and enjoy a vacation at a little cost. Lots of good milk, cream, butter and eggs and fruits in their season.

Algoma may be said to be a succession of lakes, streams and rivers abounding in fish of all kinds. In the fall there is shooting of various kinds in many parts of the District.

In winter this country is the paradise of the snow shoer, tobboganist, and as for sleighing there is generally good sleighing from early in the winter until late in the spring.

Read the following from recent "colonization notes" in the "Sault Express."

In Algoma we have a climate which may truthfully be said to be very good. In speaking of climate one has to speak relatively.

As there is no country in the world which has not its disadvantages and drawbacks, so there is no climate which is perfect—which has not its faults.

There are some parts of the world—many of them—where the climate is not good, where it is not healthful, in some where it is very bad.

Taking Canada as a whole, the climate is good; probably the Province of Ontario is favored in this respect more than the other Provinces, and Algoma, being the North West part of Ontario, "The New Ontario," "The New North West," we have, in common with the rest of the residents of Ontario, the many advantages of a good climate. But our climate here in Algoma has advantages which persons resident in Lower Ontario do not enjoy. Even in the hottest part of the summer, our night are cool and refreshing.

And our winter seasons are not changeable; from the time when once they set in, in earnest, about the middle of December or Christmas time, until about the middle of March, one can generally count on having steady winter weather. And the winter weather here is so agreeable, with the exception, perhaps, of only two or three days all season. The winter days are sunny, clear, cold, bright days. One thing we have in Algoma *par excellence* and that is good snow for sleighing and snow shoeing all winter. The snow is a valuable element in Algoma, it falls early in December, and stays till about the end of March. It does not, as in other counties, melt away during the winter, and change to mud.

The snow is worth thousands of dollars to the people in Algoma in connection with the lumber industry alone. Extensive lumbering operations are being carried on every winter; large quantities of pine, paper wood, (fibre wood, balsam and spruce, out of which paper *papier mache* is manufactured.) cedar, tamarac, hard wood, birch and maple are got out every winter by lumbermen all over the District, for Algoma is thickly wooded with all kinds of merchantable and valuable timber. And if it were not for the snow these lumbering operations could not be carried on.

To get out the wood without the snow would cost thousands of dollars extra every winter. During the winter lumbermen and others can drive with sleighs in and out of roads which would, of course, be impassable but for the snow.

In the lower portions of Ontario, and in other parts of Canada, one cannot depend on the sleighing; in Algoma you can count on sleighing and snow all winter.

Then, again, what a great thing to the farmer the snow is from the protection it affords for fall wheat.

One reason why you can grow such excellent fall wheat in Algoma is that the snow falls early in the winter or late in the fall, and covers the ground and protects the fall wheat from all danger of frost. This is a point in favor of Algoma which should be considered.

In the Western States and Territories they have snow, but it is not the right kind, either to make good sleighing or snow shoeing, or to cover the fall wheat. It is composed of fine particles like granulated sugar; it won't "pack" or "settle," but blows all over like sand. It blows right off the road, right off the field, and leaves the ground bare, and that is why, when the wind gets up in the Western States and Territories, they have such dreadful blizzards.

The worst of prairie life is that you are at the mercy of the wind. Any little commotion in the air is to be dreaded in Western States and Dakota. What would be a little zephyr playing among the trees in Algoma, means a deadly " blizzard " there, because, there being no timber or real timber, only what we would call brush or furze, the country has no chance against the wind, no protection, and when a little wind, a baby wind, gets up to play, the further it goes and the longer it blows the stronger it gets, and in a few minutes it is, if in winter, a blizzard, and in summer a hurricane, and carries destruction and loss of life in its wake.

In summer, these storms are very destructive to property, and sometimes to life, but they are more dangerous in winter on account of the densely blinding snow and the extreme freezing cold.

LANDS IN ALGOMA—WHERE AND HOW TO OBTAIN THEM. ONTARIO FREE GRANT AND TWENTY CENTS AN ACRE LANDS AND DOMINION INDIAN (SURRENDERED) LANDS.

There are all over the north shore and the Islands of Manitoulin, Cockburn and St. Joseph, dozens and scores of townships containing thousands of acres of as fine arable, agricultural, fruit growing and stock raising lands as can be found in the world, and which can be obtained by the actual settler, free, or almost free, from the Crown Lands Department of Ontario, or the Indian Department of the Dominion Government. We advise anyone interested in these Free Grant or Indian Lands to write to the Crown Lands Department at Toronto, enclosing $1, for the large map of "The North Shore of Lake Huron," issued by that Department in 1890, or a later edition if there is one. This map is about 4 ft. 6 in. x 2 ft. 6 in., and shows the Indian townships painted Red, so that the Indian townships can easily be distinguished from the Ontario townships. On looking at it, it will be observed that all the townships on the Manitoulin and Cockburn are Indian lands, also the fertile townships of Dennis and Pennefather, and several other townships north, west and east of Sault Ste. Marie on the main land, and that the lands on St. Joseph Island are Ontario Crown lands, also in Prince and several other Twps. on the north shore.

There are besides the townships which are surveyed thousands of acres to the north of them owned by the Governments which are not surveyed, and as fast as the townships which are now open to location are taken up by settlers, the Governments will open other townships for location as they are needed.

There is room on the fertile lands lying to the north of Lakes Huron and Superior and the river St. Mary, and on the Islands of Manitoulin, Cockburn and St. Joseph, and owned by the Dominion and the Ontario Governments respectively, for the surplus population not only of Older Canada, but of Europe. Then in addition there is Balfour and other townships in Algoma East, and Oliver and other townships in Algoma West on the main line of the C. P. R.

Information as to the Ontario and Free Grant and 20 cents an acre lands can be obtained from the Crown Lands Department at Toronto, or from the following and other Local Crown Lands agents in the District of Algoma.

The Crown Lands Agents resident at Sault Ste. Marie, Richard's Landing, Thessalon or Massey. Information as to the several townships of Indian Lands open for location may be obtained from the Department of Indian affairs at Ottawa, or the following local Indian Land Agents in Algoma. The Indian Agents resident at Sault Ste. Marie, Thessalon, Manitowaning or Cockburn Island or at the offices of the Agent of the Ontario Government in Liverpool, England, or of the Dominion Government at London, England, or elsewhere in Great Britain. Any agent or friend of the A. L. & C. Co. in or out of Algoma will also cheerfully give any information in his power both as to Ontario or Indian Lands to any intending settler.

There is room for the landless folks and the homeless folks of the world on these Free Grant and 20 cent an acre and Indian lands. Nobody need be afraid to come thinking there is not room for him or her in Algoma on these Government lands; as fast as the present townships are located the Governments will open up fresh townships of equally good land.

Desirable improved, partially improved and wild lands in the front and settled and partially settled townships of the District:

At the outset of the immigration and colonization movement in Algoma, it was felt that something would have to be done about the large tracts of magnificent land owned by speculators, syndicates and companies situate all over the District, and then many of the settlers also were holding for speculation blocks of land which they did not need and could not work themselves. And then also it was felt that a good many of the new settlers coming to Algoma would have a little capital or means, and would much prefer to buy a desirable farm either improved, partially improved or wild, and situate within one of the front and settled or partially settled townships than to go further back from the present settlements, and take up Free Grant 20 cents an acre or Indian Land.

Doubtless, owing to the impetus, this present Immigration and Colonization movement is giving to the settlement of the country, many of the townships in which there is not at present a single settler will be well settled inside of the next five years and have municipal institutions and good schools, churches, etc.; and we think no settler need be afraid when he goes back into the new townships but that he will soon have lots of company.

But it was felt by the friends of the "movement" that it would be a step in the right direction if as much as possible of these vacant lands, situate in the front and settled and partially settled townships, and now held largely for speculation and lying vacant, idle and unproductive, could be got into the hands of this Company for the purposes of actual settlement.

The Board are glad to say that after several months hard work they have succeeded in some measure in their attempt in this direction, and the following list and particulars of desirable improved, partially improved and wild lands in the front, settled and partially settled townships, shows what they have accomplished in this direction.

The Board wish here to express their hearty thanks to and appreciation of the efforts of the agents and friends of the Company all over the district who have aided in getting these desirable, vacant and idle lands into the Company's hands for the purpose of actual settlement, and trust they will continue their labors so that within the next year or two we may be able to say that there is not an acre of farm land in Algoma held idle or unproductive, or for purposes of speculation. Lists and particulars of lands subsequently acquired by the Company's agents will, from time to time, be published in the Company's pamphlets and the attention of the world thus directed to them.

The owners or holders of all vacant or idle agricultural or stock raising lands in Algoma, no matter where such owners or holders may reside, are asked at once to communicate with the Company's Secretary and put their lands at once into the Company's hands for the purpose of actual settlement so that they can appear in our next list.

Our agents have made a report of these lands according to forms "B" and "C" as follows:

FORM B.

Parcel Number——in the Company's books. Description of lands. 1. Number of acres cleared. 2. Number of acres uncleared. 3. Buildings: State character and dimensions of house, barn, stable, root-house, driving sheds, etc., etc. 4. How farm watered: Springs, creeks, wells. 5. Is the farm particularly adapted for sheep raising, or how many acres for that purpose? 6. Is the farm particularly adapted for cattle raising, or how many acres for that purpose? 7. Is the farm particularly adapted for grain raising, or for the growing of roots, or for fruit culture, or for general agriculture? Remarks. 8. State character of soil. 9. State character and kind of timber and estimated amount. 10. State names of nearest towns, villages and settlements, and distances from each. 11. Name of nearest post office and distance. 12. Churches, (Protestant and Catholic) including religious services regularly held in school houses, etc., distances. 13. Nearest public school, distance. 14. Roads: How far from leading road or roads. 15. How far from nearest steamship port. 16. How far from railroad. 17. State anything not included in above which may be of interest or importance connected with the farm or neighborhood.

FORM C.

CONFIDENTIAL—Please state confidentially for the information of the Board of Directors and the Company's Agents : 1. What to the best of your information, skill and knowledge, and to the best of your opinion, are worth per acre: The cleared land; the uncleared land. 2. What to the best of your opinion are the buildings on the farm worth in all and separately ? 3. What to the best of your information, skill and knowledge and to the best of your opinion is the farm worth at a fair and reasonable price? 4. What is the very lowest price at which in your opinion, the land should be sold by the Company, having regard to the fact that the Company is desirous to settle Algoma and wishes to sell its wild, improved and partially improved farms at low prices to its purchasers.

The reader is requested to call on or correspond with the Local Agent whose name is printed opposite each parcel of land, and he will be happy to give or write any further information about the land or its price, and if the reader wants a copy of form "B" relating to any land he can write to the Company's Secretary.

Do not be afraid to correspond either with the Company's Local Agents or with the Secretary as to any land in our lists, or as to any Free Grant 20 cents an acre, or Indian Land anywhere in Algoma.

Our agents are supplied with a form of Agreement of bargain or sale, (form H) which the purchaser will sign at the time of closing the sale with the agent or the Company; at the time of signing the Agreement, the purchaser will also pay into or remit to one of the Chartered Banks at Sault Ste. Marie, a deposit of 10% of the purchase price as an evidence of good faith, such deposit to be put to the Company's credit in said bank.

Probably in most cases the sales will be made and arranged by correspondence between the settler and the Company or its local agent, before the settler moves here. The agents in the Old Country of the Company's bankers are given on the cover, and remittances can of course be made through them.

All lands placed in the Company's hands for settlement will be sold very cheap to actual settlers at prices far below their real value. Write the local agent as to the prices or the secretary.

Directions as to payment of monies to the Company may be found in By-Laws

Nos. 6 and 7 printed on the co 'er of this pamphlet, and to which public attention is here called.

As to terms: In nearly every case, there can be in the agreement of bargain of sale, (form H) a provision for deferred payments, for a large proportion of the purchase money being paid by instalments spread over a term of years with very low interest on the principal remaining unpaid.

Even though these farms are offered to actual settlers at prices far below their real value, yet if the incoming settlers buying them had to pay all the price down in cash at the time of purchase, it might inconvenience them or some of them, and prevent them from getting as good a start in Algoma as they otherwise would make.

We would like as many as possible of the settlers who come to Algoma, to fetch some good stock with them from Lower Ontario or Quebec or elsewhere.

This work surely contains sufficient evidence to prove Algoma is par-excellence, a cattle country, a sheep country, a hog country, and a dairying country, but so far there is a great dearth of good improved stock in the District. Do not be afraid to fetch good stock with you to Algoma; if you are in doubt as to what kind to fetch, correspond with our local agent nearest to the township in which you are settling, or with the president or secretary of the nearest township branch agricultural society, or with the president or secretary of the Eastern Algoma Electoral District Agricultural Society, or with the president or secretary cf either the Eastern Algoma Farmer's Institute or the Central Algoma Farmer's Institute, and get their opinion. The farmers in Algoma at all their meetings lately have been discussing the stock question, and have arrived at this phase of it: If poor cattle, scrub cattle do so wel' in Algoma what would good cattle do here! If there is lots of money in the business with poor cattle, how much more would there be with good cattle!

The North Shore Navigation Company (Ld.) have promised not only very cheap transportation rates for freight and passengers to settlers moving into the District, but cheap tourist and land explorers tickets to all points in Algoma. Their steamers sail from Collingwood, Meaford, Owen Sound and Wiarton; for folders address W. J. Sheppard, Gen. Mgr., Waubaushene, Ont. or C. E. Stephen, Collingwood.

The C. P. R. Co. are issuing land explorers tickets at reduced rates to settlers moving into the District from any point on their lines in Ontario east of Sharbut Lake Junction and in Quebec, to any point in Algoma, between Mattawa Ont. on the Ottawa River, and Missanabie on the main line, or Garden River on the Soo Line. (For these reduced rates application should be made to L. O. Armstrong, Coln. Agt. C. P. R., Montreal. We trust the other steamship and railway companies will do the same, and allow us so to announce in our next edition and future pamphlets.

☞ The company does not of course guarantee anything, or make any warranty as to any lands placed in their hands for settlement. We simply publish extracts from the particulars as given to us, and do not in any case warrant their correctness.

We will be glad in all cases to send free to any enquirer a copy of form "B", and to give any other information in our power relating to any land placed in our hands for settlement. People are asked to call on or correspond direct with our local agents about the lands. They are all prominent and well known men in their vicinities, and will be happy to give full information about any land to any one writing them or calling on them.

Parcel 1. S w ¼ sec. 9, Prince. 20 acres cleared, 140 uncleared, hewed log house, plastered inside and out, 18x22, two storeys; log barn 26x26, log stable 20x16; well at house, never failing spring, good soil. 5, 6 and 7, yes. 8, clay loam; 9, mixed merchantable birch, maple, oak, pine, cedar, valuable timber. 15 miles to

Sault Ste. Marie, Korah P. O. 6 m. School to be in settlement by 1st Nov. (See letter in EXPRESS referring to this township.)

Parcel 2. S e ¼ sec. 9 Prince. 25 acres cleared, 135 uncleared, good hewed log house well shingled, plastered inside and out 24x18, 1½ storey, log stables etc., temporary sheep house, etc., never failing spring creek through centre. 5, 6 and 7, yes; owner says never had a bad crop on it. 8, clay loam. 9, hard wood maple, oak, pine, cedar, birdseye maple; merchantable hardwood, large amount. 14 m. to Sault Ste. Marie.

Parcel 3. S w ¼ sec. 1, Parke. 8 acres cleared, 152 uncleared, frame of a building 18x20, 8 m to Sault Ste. Marie, 4 m to Korah P. O. Sandy loam and black loam. No stone; all the wood valuable, tamarack, poplar, cedar, spruce, white birch etc. Most of the farm lies high, a few acres low; easily drained.

Parcel 4. S e ¼ sec. 11, Parke. 160 acres all timbered. 4. Little lake. 5, 6 and 7, yes. 8. Sandy loam. 9. Mixed. 8 m Sault Ste. Marie, 1 m Point aux Pins. Prettily situated. 3 acres of a lake on it, whole lake about 10 acres, only 40 rods from St. Mary's River. Excellent for strawberries and general crops.

Parcel 5. N e ¼ sec. 3 Parke, 160 acres all timbered. 4, spring creek in front. 5, 6 and 7, yes. 8, Sandy loam. 9. Mixed. 8 m to Sault Ste. Marie, 3 to Point aux Pins. Excellent soil.

Parcel 6. S e ¼ sec. 32 Laird. 40 acres cleared, 120 uncleared, small log house about 10x24, good repair, log barn about 30x36 good repair. 4. Spring creek across farm, also well, spring water at door, pump. 5, 6, 7, yes. 8. Clay loam. 9. Mixed, valuable. Port Finlay 4m, Maclennan 1 m, Bruce Mines 17, in centre of good settlement, very desirable farm. Local agent Wm. Murray, Bar River P. O.

Parcel 7. Lot 22, con. 12, Billings. 6 cleared, 94 uncleared, log shanty, habitable, good root house, log barn, stable attached to side. Never failing spring. West Bay 6 m, Kagawong 4 m; prospects good for stock farmer. Sandy loam. Local agent, T. Bowser, Kagawong.

Parcel 8. N ½ lot 2, con. 3, Plummer. 30 acres cleared, 117½ uncleared, good house 16x20. 4. Creek. 5, 6, 7, yes. Sandy loam. Mixed timber, pine, cedar, hemlock, maple, etc., on main road. Govt. road on two sides of it. Rydal Bank 1 mile, in good settlement. Local agent W. R. Smythe, Rydal Bank.

Parcel 9. S w pt. lot 10, con. 4, Day. 50 acres cleared, 100 uncleared, frame house 18x26 and 16x18, frame barn 36x56, granary 16x18. Good well with pump. Spring creek. Clay loam. Mixed timber. Thessalon Ry. Sta. 8 m, Dayton Sta. 8 m, Sowerby 3 m. This is said to be a first-class farm; new frame buildings valued for insurance at $1200. Local agent W. L. Nichols, Thessalon.

Parcel 10. W ½ lot 3, con. 6, Plummer additional, 40 acres cleared, 134 uncleared, log house 22x24 good repair, frame barn 32x24. Good well. Either stock or grain farming. Clay loam. Mixed timber. Bruce Mines 4 m, Rydal Bank 1½ m. 2 m from Ry. sta. Local agent W. L. Nichols, Thessalon.

Parcel 11. S ½ lot 4, con. 1, Coffin. 20 acres cleared, 140 uncleared, shanty and small stable. 4. Lake front and spring. Part clay loam, part sandy loam. Mixed timber. Rydal Bank 6 m. Beautifully situated on Rock Lake. Local agent W. R. Smythe, Rydal Bank.

Parcel 12—W ½ lot 21, Thompson, 6 acres cleared, 10 chopped ready to log, 304 uncleared ; 4, springs ; 5, yes, or cattle raising or grain ; part sandy loam, part clay ; mixed timber, birch, cedar, tamarac, hemlock and spruce. Railway runs across lot, station 1¼ miles on Government road. Local Agent—W. L. Nichols, Thessalon.

Parcel 13—W ½ lot 20, Thompson, 320 acres uncleared ; same as above ; station ½ mile ; Thompson post office ½ mile. Local Agent—W. L. Nichols, Thessalon.

Parcel 14—E ½ lot 20, Thompson, 25 acres cleared and 15 chopped and burned ready to log, 280 uncleared. Barn 30x44, log ; house 24x40, with wing 18x24, frame ; well and springs. Cattle, sheep or mixed farming. Mixed timber ; on Government road ; railway station on lot. Local Agent—W L. Nichols, Thessalon.

Parcel 15—N w ¼ section 19, Thompson, 160 acres uncleared. 4.Springs. Sheep, cattle or grain ; sandy loam, portion clay loam ; C. P. R. crosses lot 1½ miles from steamship port. W. L. Nichols, Thessalon.

Parcel 16—N ½ s e ¼ lot 16, Tarentorus 30 acres cleared, 50 uncleared. Good hewed log house ; good log barn, stable and outhouses. 4. Good spring creek and well. Good for grain, cattle, roots and fruit ; loamy soil ; mixed timber, valuable ; in good settlement ; Sault Ste. Marie 5½ miles.

Parcel 17—S e ¼ section 6, Tarentorus, 160 acres. 4. Creek. Sandy loam ; cattle, grain and fruit ; thickly timbered with birch and maple ; said to be sufficient hardwood done to realize a very large sum. Sault Ste. Marie 7 miles.

Parcel 18—S ½ s w ¼ section 17, Macdonald, 6 acres cleared and fenced with cedar rails and wire fence, 63 uncleared. Good well ; cattle, sheep, grain, fruit, general ; good soil. Echo Bay railway station 20 rods ; Echo Bay post office on corner lot ; good location for dairy ; whole 63 acres can be ploughed ; land easily cleared ; splendid gardening soil ; in heart of settlement. Expected there will be a village at Echo Bay station in near future. W. Finlay, Echo Bay ; or A. Finlay, Echo River.

Parcel 19—E ½ s w ¼ section 16, Macdonald, 30 acres cleared, 50 uncleared. Hewed log house 22x16 ; double log barn ; good root house ; buildings insured for $400 ; good well ; splendid crops raised. Maple, birch, oak and basswood, estimated large amount. Echo Bay station 1¼ miles ; Echo River 1¼ miles. Beautiful view of Lake George and River St. Mary. Cedar posts and wire fence around three-fourths of 30 acres cleared ; on Lake Shore road. Local Agents—W. Finlay, Echo Bay ; or A. Finlay, Echo River.

Parcel 20—W ½ s w ¼ section 15, Macdonald, 5 acres cleared, 75 uncleared. 4. Spring creek ; good general farm ; sheep, cattle, roots, grain, fruits ; clay loam ; mixed timber, valuable. Echo River ½ mile ; Echo Bay station 2½ miles ; fronting on two roads. Local Agents—W. Finlay, Echo Bay ; or A. Finlay, Echo River.

Parcel 21—N ½ n e ¼ and n ½ n w ¼ section 10, Macdonald, 160 acres.' Fronts on Echo river ; spring on property. Good land for general purposes, grain, fruit, stock or roots ; would make two good farms of 80 acres each ; contains large amount valuable hardwood, birch, maple and merchantable oak ; 4 miles to Echo Bay station ; on Echo River road. Estimated value of timber standing very large. Tugs can run up the river past farm ; handy place to ship timber by water ; 1½ miles south of Echo Lake. Fair showing of iron on a bluff on property. Local Agents—W. Finlay, Echo Bay ; or A. Finlay, Echo River.

Parcel 22—S e ¼ of n e ¼ section 35 and s w ¼ n w ¼ section 36, Macdonald, 80 acres uncleared ; 4. Bar River runs through it. 5, 6, 7, yes, all. Clay loam ; 1½ miles from Isbester station, 6 from Echo Bay ; in heart of good settlement ; good water power on lot ; lot easily cleared, logs being burnt off ; only small trouble to clear ; can be ploughed immediately after. Local Agents—W. Finlay, Echo Bay ; or A. Finlay, Echo River.

Parcel 23—Lots 7 and 8, con 9, Cockburn Island, 22 acres cleared, 178 uncleared. Hewed log barn 24x34 and stables attached. 4. Spring creek and well. 5. 6, 7, yes. An orchard planted, commencing to bear ; about 20 apple trees. 9 Birch, maple, hemlock, cedar, tamarac and beech. Tolsonville 2 miles ; on leading road ; can be divided into 2 or more good farms. In addition to 22 acres cleared there is a quantity burnt land easily cleared, well situated, splendid view of lake. Local Agent—W. J. Harper, Cockburn Island.

Parcel 24—N w ¼ section 15, Lefroy —35 acres cleared, 125 uncleared ; house, log, 17x22 and 16x17 ; barn 20x46, frame post. 4.Good well, river and spring. Good for cattle, grain, roots, etc.; clay loam. Thessalon 9 miles, on good leading road. Local Ag nt—W. L. Nichols, Thessalon.

Parcel 25. N e ¼ sec. 27 and s e corner n w ¼ sec. 27, Lefroy, 50 cleared, well fenced, cedar rails, 129 uncleared, 30 acres hardwood bush, balance burnt land, easily cleared. Good hewed log house 25x18 and 25x12. Hewed log barn 50x28 with stable underneath for 30 head of cattle, do, cedar log 25x25, good well and creek. Cattle, sheep, general farming, clay loam. 6 miles from Thessalon, 8 miles from Bruce Mines, 3 miles from station. Local agent W. L. Nichols, Thessalon.

Parcel 26. S ¼ lot 11, do, lot 12, Bridgland, 26 cleared, 294 uncleared. 4. Good creek. Cattle, sheep, fruit and grain. Sandy loam, mixed timber. Thessalon 9 miles, Little Rapids 5 miles. Leading road touches s w corner lot 12. Would make 2 or 3 good farms. Local agent W. L. Nichols, Thessalon.

Parcel 27. N ½ s e ¼ sec. 37 Haviland, 15 cleared, 65 uncleared. 4. Good spring creek. 5. yes. 6. yes. 7. ½ well adapted for grain, ½ better adapted for roots and stock raising. 8. Clay loam. 9. Pine, spruce, maple, birch, cedar, balsam. Sault Ste. Marie 18 m on leading road. Goulais Bay P. O. ¼ m. Well situated, valuable timber. 2 m from Batchewana Bay. Local agent A. McAuley, Goulais Bay.

Parcel 28. N e ¼ sec. 12 Fenwick, 55 cleared, 95 uncleared. Good hewed log house 18x28, hewed log barn 20x60, granary, spring at foot of mountain. 5, 6, 7, yes; 20 acres light loam, 20 yellow loam, balance clay loam. Maple, birch, balsam, cedar. In centre of Goulais Bay settlement, Sault Ste. Marie 24 m on leading road. Clear of stone. 1½ m to Goulais Bay P. O. This is a first-class farm. Local agent A. McAuley, Goulais Bay.

Parcel 29. S e ¼ sec. 1 Fenwick, 36 acres cleared, 114 uncleared ; house hewed log 1½ storeys 20x26, stable 20x30. 4. One well, several springs. Well adapted for all kinds of grain, fruit, roots, stock. Clay loam, mixed timber, valuable. Sault Ste. Marie 17 m, Goulais Bay P. O. 1 m, school house and church adjoining, 2½ m from Goulais Bay, 3½ from Batchewana Bay either which likely to become a port in the near future. Local agent A. McAuley, Goulais Bay.

Parcel 30. S ½ lot 4, con. 4 Kirkwood, 25 cleared, 135 uncleared, house hewed logs 18x24, barn log 42x24. 4. Well. 5, 6, 7, yes. Sandy loam. Birch and maple. Thessalon 8 m, Little Rapids 4 m on leading road. Local agent W. L. Nicholas, Thessalon.

Parcel 31. Lot 1 con. 9 St. Joseph Island, 30 cleared, 70 uncleared, house 24x30 1½ storey, new, cost $650. log barn 20x30, stable and root house, spring creek. 5, 6, 7, yes. Sandy loam. Birch, maple, beech and cedar. Marksville 7 m, on leading road, 11 m to railway. Local agent S. T. Bowker, Marksville.

Parcel 32. Lots 8 and 9 con. m do, two good farms, 40 cleared, 160 uncleared, house 24x30, barn 60x30, 2 stables, 2 root houses, well with pump. 5, 6, 7, yes. Dark gravelly loam. Chiefly maple. Valuable. Excellent crops raised. Marksville 6 m, Jocelyn 6 m. Local agent W. Williamson Jocelyn.

Parcel 33. Lot 16 con. K, do, 25 cleared, 75 uncleared, house 16x24, barn and stable 43x21. Creek. 5, 6, 7, yes. Clay loam. Cedar, hemlock, hardwood. Marksville 3½ m, leading road. Local agent, S. T. Bowker, Marksville.

Parcel 34. Lot 19, con. K, do, 10 acres cleared, 90 uncleared. House 20x26, stable 18x20. Creek. 5, 6, 7, yes. Clay loam. 50 acres maple, balance mixed. Marksville 3½ m. Local agent, S. T. Bowker, Marksville.

Parcel 35. Lots 3 and 4, con. 13, do, 2 or more good farms, 5 acres cleared, 75 almost cleared, 120 uncleared. 5, 6, 7, yes. Fruit particularly. All District good for cattle and sheep. Sandy loam. Sugar maple, black birch, basswood, timber very valuable. Marksville 1 mile, 7 miles from Ry. Sta. This land was fit for seeding April 4th this year. Local Agent H. E. Bishop, Marksville.

Parcel 36. Lot 5, con. 1, do, 2 acres cleared, 97 acres uncleared, 25 acres for cattle raising, 74 general agriculture, rich sandy loam, 74 acres maple and beech, balance pine and mixed. 12 miles to Hilton, 2 miles to Tenby Bay. Schoolhouse on lot. 18 m to Ry. Sta. Good market for cordwood within 2 m. Corner lot. Local agent W. Williamson, Jocelyn.

Parcel 37. Lot 18, con. L, do, 4 cleared, 85 uncleared. Log house 16x20. Spring. 5, 6, 7, yes. 30 acres maple balance mixed. Marksville 4 m, on leading road. Ry. Sta. 6 miles. Steamship port 4 miles. Local agent, S. T. Bowker, Marksville.

Parcel 38. Lot 6, con. N, do, 8 cleared, 92 uncleared. Shanty. Spring. 5, 6, 7, yes. Rich sandy loam. Maple, basswood and birch. Hilton 7 m, Jocelyn 2½ m, Richards Landing 7 m, Carterton 1 m, school ½ m. Corner lot. Local agent, W. Williamson, Jocelyn.

Parcel 39. Lots 22 and 23, con. XIV, do, would make two or three good farms. 18 acres cleared, 176 uncleared. Small log house. Spring creek. 5, 6, 7, yes. Clay loam. Cedar and maple. Marksville 5½ m, leading road. Local agent, E. Stubbs, Marksville.

Parcel 40. Lot 4, con. 16, do, 16 cleared, 84 mixed timber, spring and creek. 5, 6, 7, yes. Clay & sandy loam, all clear of stone. Marksville 1½ m, leading road. Local agent, S. T. Bowker, Marksville.

Parcel 41. Lots 1 and 2, con. 17, do, 100 cleared, 97 uncleared, would make 2 or 3 good farms. Log house 18x24, barn 24x34. Spring creek. 5, 6, 7, yes. Sandy loam. Timber very valuable, hardwood. Marksville ½ mile. Local agent, S. T. Bowker, Marksville.

Parcel 42. Lot 23, con. 8, do, 121 acres, small house 16x20 (log). Spring creek. Clear of stone. 5, 6, 7, yes. Mixed timber, very valuable. Marksville 2 m. Local agent, S. T. Bowker, Marksville.

Parcel 43. Lot 20, con. L, do, 10 cleared, 100 well timbered. Spring creek. 5, 6, 7, yes. Clay loam, clear of stone. Mixed timber, very valuable. Marksville 2 m. Local agent, S. T. Bowker, Marksville.

Parcel 44. Lot 28, con. A, do, 15 cleared, 85 burnt land easily cleared. Spring and creek. 5, 6, 7, yes. Clay loam, enough cedar for fencing, and hardwood for firewood. Hilton 10 m. Richards Landing 7 m, Sea Gull 5 m. Church on corner lot. Local agent, S. T. Bowker, Marksville.

Parcel 45. S w ¼, sec 7 Vankoughnet, 20 acres cleared, 185 uncleared, house 1½ storeys high, 24x22, log, hewed inside, barn 30x58, hewed log stable 12x18, do 20x18, root house 10x24, milk house and kitchen 18x20. 4. Springs. 5, 6, 7, yes. Clay loam. 9. Chiefly hardwood, valuable. Sault Ste. Marie 17 miles, Goulais Bay P.O. ¾ mile. On leading road. A bluff of slate extends into and occupies some few acres. Indications of mineral. Local agent, A. McAuley, Goulais Bay.

Parcel 46. S ½, s e ¼, sec 7, do, 23 acres cleared, 57 uncleared, barn 52x26 hewed log, new hewed log house 21x25, 1½ storeys high, stable 14x18 hewed inside, root house. Very well watered spring and creek. 5, 6, 7, yes. Fine clay loam, a small portion a little gravelly. 9. Chiefly hardwood. 17 m S. S. Marie, Goulais Bay P. O. 1¾ m. Free from stone, gently rolling, pretty site. Local agent, A. McAuley, Goulais Bay.

Parcel 47. W ½ n w ¼, 7 do, 43 cleared, 62 uncleared, hewed log house 1½ storeys high, 18x24, barn log 24x36, 1 stable 16x30, do 12x26, root house etc. Spring creek on each end. 5, 6, 7, yes. Clay loam. 9. Principally hardwood, some spruce and balsam. S. S. Marie 18 m. P. O. ½ m, 3 m Goulais Bay, 5 m Batchewana Bay either of which may be a port in near future. Mineral discovered some 2 m distant. Local agent, A. McAuley, Goulais Bay.

Parcel 48. N e ¼ sec 18, do, 20 acres cleared, 124 acres uncleared, house 16x22, 1½ storeys, stoop attached, barn 18x26. Well watered creek and springs. 5, 6, 7, yes. Clay loam. 9. Chiefly hardwood. 1 m from P. O. S. S. Marie 17 m easy distance from Goulais and Batchewana Bays. Local agent, A. McAuley, Goulais Bay.

Parcel 49. N ½ n e ¼ sec 19, do, 89 acres, chiefly hardwood. 4. Springs 5, 6, 7, yes. Part clay loam, part sandy loam. 16 m S. S. Marie, Goulais Bay P. O. 2½ miles. Convenient to well settled neighborhood. Would make a good farm. Local agent, A. McAuley, Goulais Bay.

Parcel 50. W ½, s w ¼ of s e ¼, sec 5, Tarentorus, 20 acres, s ½ s w ¼ sec 5, do, 80 acres, in all 100 acres some 10 acres cleared, about 5 partly cleared, timber valuable hardwood. About 6 miles from S. S. Marie. 5, 6, 7, yes. Would make excellent dairy, stock raising or general purpose farm. Watered by trout stream on property, other creeks close. Prettily situated.

Parcel 51. S w ¼ sec 10, Prince, hewed log house, log stable, 160 acres, 25 to 30 acres cleared, balance principally hardwood valuable, good soil. 5, 6, 7, yes. (See Prince letter from Express.) About 13 miles to S. S. Marie. Spring Creek on property.

Parcel 52. N e ¼ s e ¼ sec 24, Prince, 33¼ acres, timbered. All good for pasture, sheep and cattle, and some few acres for general agriculture. Timber said to be valuable. Bluff supposed to contain mineral. About 6 m from S. S. Marie.

Parcel 53. W ½ s w ¼ sec 17, Korah, 80 acres. 5, 6, 7, yes. Timber hardwood, cedar, [illegible]. Good road leading to n w corner post. Has a fine cranberry marsh of about 20 acres covered with [illegible] and balsam. A dam could be built on creek where it crosses e and w line between secs 17 and 20 to flood marsh [illegible] suit weather and growth cranberry crop. Soil just what is required. 60 acres grain, roots, fruit or stock. 20 acres marsh if drained would also make very best of land any purpose. Sault Ste. Marie 7½ miles. Prettily situated.

Parcel 54. N e ¼ n e ¼ sec 20, Korah, 40 acres 6 m from S. S. Marie. Well watered spring creek. Sandy loam. 5, 6, 7, yes in part. Timbered with hardwood and other timber, water power could easily be had on this lot. Would make a good farm for man of small means when cleared and got into shape. Could not be beaten for grazing, dairy or sheep and still have lots of land left for good market garden. Convenient to town and school, bluff on this property supposed to contain mineral but has not been explored.

Parcel 55. W ½ s e ¼ sec 18, Korah, 80 acres, 7 m from S. S. Marie. Good road. About 10 acres suitable for cranberry marsh, right soil and fine creek. About 10 acres of hardwood, valuable, 60 acres spruce, tamarac, cedar, 70 acres well suited for grain, roots fruit and stock. If marsh (10 acres) drained would be excellent for any purpose well situated.

Parcel 56. N w ¼ sec 4, Korah, 160 acres well watered, valuable hardwood, merchantable and other timber. Stony ridge of few acres along Goulais Bay road, (see Pennefather letter) excellent for pasture, cattle or sheep could not be better for that purpose. Some few acres on ridge already cleared, balance of land free of stone rich soil, grain, roots, fruit, excellent for stock, very well watered. S. S. Marie 8 miles.

Parcel 57. S e ¼ s e ¼ sec 10, do, 40 acres, valuable hardwood, good soil, grain, fruit cattle, sheep. Market gardening. Would make excellent farm for man with small means when cleared and got into shape. Prettily situated on inland lake. S. S. Marie 6½ miles.

Parcel 58. N w ¼ sec 10, Parke, 160 acres. Mixed timber. 5, 6, 7, yes. For fruit cannot be excelled. Easily cleared, would make good farm any purpose. Point aux Pines 2 miles. S. S. Marie 8 miles. Well watered.

Parcel 59. S. w ¼ sec 14 Vankoughnet, 152 acres, mixed timber, valuable pulp wood and other timber. Contains some excellent land for grain, fruit, roots, and would make an excellent stock farm when cleared. In the fertile Goulais District. Well watered. Goulais Bay 4 miles. Local agent, A. McAuley, Goulais Bay.

Parcel 60. Lot No. 1 (Keatings plan) 400 acres, Lot D (Wilsons plan) 295 acres. In fertile valley Batchewaung River. This river is easterly boundary. In a few years doubtless this valley will be thickly settled. Several Twps. all round (Ontario and Dom.) open for location. Probably half of 700 acres could not be beaten for grain, roots, fruit etc. when cleared and brought into cultivation. Other half could not be beaten for stock and sheep raising. Some bluffs on land supposed to contain mineral. The whole 700 acres coverd with valuable hardwood. Merchantable birch and maple. Road constructed, 4 m to dock on Batchewaung Bay, deep water, timber could be got out that way, or mill built either on property or at Bay. Hardwood very valuable either for merchandise or as cordwood at S. S. Marie, Mich. or Ont. This 700 acres could be divided into several farms.

Parcel 61. Block Q, Garden River, Indian Reserve, North Echo Lake, 218 acres, some excellent land for general agricultural purposes, balance pasture land. Some valuable timber. Some bluffs on property supposed to contain iron. 1 1-10 m n e head of Echo Lake. (Surrendered portion reserve.)

Parcel 62. N w ¼, 20 Lefroy, 160 acres, hardwood, tamarac, cedar, spruce and other valuable timber. Near Ry. Would make good pasture land when cleared. Well watered. Would do well for sheep or cattle. Some good land for roots, grain and fruit. Between Bruce Mines and Thessalon, in good settlement. Said to be some valuable timber on this lot. Would make good stock farm for industrious man of small means.

Parcel 63. S w ¼, 8 Rose, 154 acres, valuable pulp wood and other timber. Contains some excellent land for grain, roots, fruit and the balance good for sheep and stock. Would make good stock farm for industrious man of small means. Rose is a good township. Local agent, Chas. Warren, Rydal Bank.

Parcel 64. S w ¼, 20, do, 160 acres. Same remarks will apply. Local agent, Chas. Warren, Rydal Bank.

Parcel 65. S ½ sec 32, Pennefather, 323 acres, about 50 acres cleared, balance hardwood, large amount merchantable, balance good cord wood. The 50 acres cleared is alongside Goulais Bay road and on stony ridge (see Pennefather letter) balance of land free of stone, splendid soil. Cleared land excellent pasture for cattle and sheep and is good hay land, balance of land cannot be excelled for grain, roots, fruit. Property lies along town line, Korah and Pennefather, former township, organized Municipality. S. S. Marie 9 miles, 8 miles when town line is completed. Now opened to within ½ to 1 mile of farm. Would make best stock farm in neighborhood. Well watered by springs and creeks. Timber valuable.

Parcel 66. S w ¼, sec 12, Lefroy, 160 acres, 20 cleared, and fenced. 5. Chopped. 130 timber, 5 acres covered by part of little inland lake. 3. House 16x22 hewed log, plastered inside and out, 1½ storeys, in good repair, barn 20x30 in good repair buildings up only about 4 years. 4. Never failing stream close to house and a little lake in one corner of the farm, this lake takes off about 5 acres, about 20 acres altogether in the lake, contains abundance of speckled trout. Stream mentioned runs into it, lake empties into Thessalon River. 5, 6, 7, yes. 8. Clay loam, good soil. 9. Maple, birch and oak, splendid maple bush, good merchantable timber, very valuable. 10. Thessalon 7, Little Rapids 1. 11. Little Rapids. 12 and 13. 1 mile. 14. On Gov. road "northern." 16. Ry. station, (Thessalon) 5 miles, in good settlement, farms all around it. Local agent, W. L. Nichols, Thessalon.

Parcel 67. Tp. Korah, lot no. 7, (21 acres) lot no. 10 (14 acres) lot no. 13, (5 acres) west of People's Road, Stewart's Survey, and n w Sub-division of sec. 36 Korah (123 acres) in all by actual measurement 168 acres.

This property is well situated for market gardeners, dairy farmers, or general farm purposes. Adjoining town of Sault Ste. Marie about 1½ miles from the centre of the town, about ½ mile from the water power canal and ship canal now in construction, said to be not an acre of waste land on farm, wood land easily cleared, a good many acres already cleared, excellent springs of water on farm, block clay loam, rich soil. Fronts on three roads; the People's road, (extension of Wellington street) the Korah road (extension of Queen street) and the Second Line. Town lots surveyed up to this farm. Low price, easy terms *en bloc* or in ten acre farm lots at low prices and according to location. (Read "Agricultural Imports into Sault Ste. Marie," ante page 56 and 57.

Parcel 68. N e ¼ sec. 34, Prince, 160 acres, 20 cleared, 140 timbered. Hewed log house 20x24 plastered inside and out. Farn 50x20, stable 20x18, buildings in good repair. 4. Spring creek and spring near house. 5, 6, 7, yes. 8. Sandy loam and clay loam. 9. Mixed pine, maple, birch, cedar, spruce, balsam. Said to be large quantity pine—other timber valuable and merchantable. Sault Ste. Marie 10 miles. 11. Korah 4 miles. 13. 1½ m. 14. on 2nd line, good leading road, Gros Cap dock, Lake Superior 4 miles, deep water, timber could be shipped there, good crops raised, excellent soil, good garden, small orchard, trees loaded this year, of the 20 acres 10 are free of stumps, would make excellent farm.

Parcel 69. Lots A and B, con. 16, St. Joseph Island, 100 acres cleared, 100 acres timber, valuable and comfortable buildings, 10 roomed house 20x30 and 18x23, 2 cellars, cupboards and all conveniences, store room and other buildings under one roof, log barn 30x60, ice house, driving shed, etc. 4. Spring in Creek with pump, several springs on property. 5, 6, 7, yes. 9. Timber very valuable. Good creek on property valuable mill site, good soil. 2 Good gardens with fruit trees bearing apples, plums, and small fruits. Could be divided into 4 or more good farms. Adjoining town plot of Marksville. Local agent, S. T. Bowker, Marksville.

Parcel 70. Lot 10 in 14th con. St. Joseph Island, 4 acres cleared, 92 timbered, log house 16x30. 4. Spring creek. 5, 6, 7, yes. 8. Clay loam. 9. About 50 acres, maple beech, black birch, balance mixed, all valuable. 10. Marksville 3 miles. 13. 1 mile. 14. On 2 main roads. 16. 8 miles, would make excellent stock farm. Local agent, H. E. Bishop, Marksville.

Parcel 71. Lot 17 in 14th con. St. Joseph Island, 20 acres cleared, 80 timbered, house, barn, stable. 4. creeks and well. 5, 6, 7, yes. 8. Clay loam, excellent soil. 9. Mixed timber valuable. 10. Marksville 4 miles. 14. "W." Line passes in front of lot. Local agent S. T. Bowker, Marksville.

Parcel 72. Lot 13 in w con. St. Joseph Island, 20 acres cleared, 80 timbered, house and barn. 4. Well. 5, 6, 7, yes. 8. Clay loam, rich. 9. Mixed timber, very valuable. 10 and 11. Marksville 4 miles. 14. Passes front of lot. 16. 3 miles. Local agent, S. T. Bowker, Marksville.

Parcel 73. Lots 11 and 12 con. 14, St. Joseph Island, 25 cleared, 102 timbered, house and barn. 4. Spring and creek. 5, 6, 7, yes. 8. Clay loam, rich. 9. Mixed timber, valuable. Marksville 2-3 miles, good roads. Local agent, S. T. Bowker, Marksville.

Parcel 74. Lot 14, con. w do 100 acres valuable timber. 5, 6, 7, yes. 8. Clay loam, rich soil. Marksville 4 miles, leading road passes in front of lot. 16. 8 miles in thriving Municipality of Hilton, could be made into excellent farm. Local agent, S. T. Bowker, Marksville.

Parcel 75. Lot 17 con. w, and lot 1 con. 18, do, 20 cleared, 200 timbered, log house 18x24, hewed inside and out, stable 18x26, shed 10x18. 4. Spring and trout stream. 5, 6, 7, yes. 8. Loam top, clay bottom. Mixed timber, valuable. 14. On main road, excellent soil, would make three or more farms. Local agent, H. E. Bishop, Marksville.

Parcel 76. N e ¼ sec. 2, Laird. 8. Cleared, seeded down, 152 timbered. 4. Spring creek in centre. 5, 6, 7, yes. 8. Clay loam, rich soil. 9. 60 acres maple and basswood, balance mixed, all valuable. Echo Bay Ry. Sta. 6 mile, lobester flag station 1 mile, Bar River P. O. ¾ mile on town line between Laird and Macdonald small bluff say 10 acres supposed to contain iron, balance 150 acres all arable. In centre of good settlement, organized Municipality. Local agents, A. Finlay, Echo River; W. Finlay, Echo Bay.

Parcel 77. Park Lot 1, con. 2 adjoining town plot S. S. Marie, 50 acres. 5, 6, 7, yes. Sandy loam, good rich soil, mixed timber, poplar, spruce, tamarac, etc., easily cleared, about 2 miles from town P. O. and Ry. Sta., adjoins Shingwauk Home farm, would make excellent farm for market gardener, dairyman or general purpose, fronts on Wellington street when opened.

Parcel 78. N ½ n e ¼ sec 22 and w ½ s e ¼ sec 15 Macdonald Twp., 159 acres, 16 cleared some years ago. 4. Spring, creek. 5, 6, 7, yes. 8. Rich clay loam. 9. Mixed, valuable, large amount of paper wood, easily cleared, 2 m Echo Bay Sta. and P. O., 2 m Echo River P. O., is in thriving settlement, farms all around it. Incorporated Municipality. Best of land for farm purpose, would make two good farms, all arable. Mining land in neighborhood. Local agent, W. Finlay, Echo Bay, A. Finlay, Echo River.

☞ Supplements to this list containing additional desirable, agricultural, fruit growing and stock raising lands will be issued from time to time as the Company have more lands placed in their hands for settlement and sale, and may be obtained from the Secretary at Sault Ste. Marie. All owners of vacant, idle farming lands anywhere in Algoma are asked to assist "The Colonization and Immigration Movement" by immediately placing their lands in our hands for the purpose of settlement. The necessary forms for the purpose may be obtained from the Secretary or from any of the local agents throughout the District. Prices must be low; it is no use any one offering us lands for settlement at high prices. They must be very low or the Executive Committee will not entertain them at all. We have already refused to consider at all scores of applications because the prices seemed high and many we have rejected when preparing this list for publication. Owners must remember this is not a speculative concern but a Colonization Co. The "object" of the Company simply is "to settle Algoma," to induce actual settlers to come and reside on the fertile agricultural, stock raising and fruit growing lands in Algoma whether they be Ontario Crown Lands or Dominion (Indian Surrendered) lands or lands placed in our hands for settlement and we are as much interested in settling the Ontario Free Grant and 20 cent an acre land and the Indian lands as we are in settling lands, placed with us for settlement. The only reason we have for taking lands in this way is that as hereinbefore explained most of the practical tenant farmers and others coming to Algoma especially those having a little means will prefer to buy land either wild, improved or partially improved in the front or settled or partially settled townships rather than go back into the Free Grant and Indian Townships.

www.ingramcontent.com/pod-product-compliance
Lightning Source LLC
Chambersburg PA
CBHW031246260626
47169CB00007B/2465